Discover more at millsandboon.co.uk.

THEIR
UNEXPECTED
BABIES

LOUISA HEATON

MILLS & BOON

First Published in Great Britain 2018
by Mills & Boon, an imprint of HarperCollins*Publishers*
1 London Bridge Street, London, SE1 9GF

© 2018 Louisa Heaton

ISBN: 978-0-263-26953-6

MIX
Paper from
responsible sources
FSC® C007454

This book is produced from independently certified FSC™ paper
to ensure responsible forest management.
For more information visit www.harpercollins.co.uk/green.

Printed and bound in Spain
by CPI, Barcelona

To Daisy

CHAPTER ONE

Dancing was an art form. There were those who could do it well, who looked as if they'd been born to dance. And there were those who did it badly—and Leah was one of them. Dancing might even be a bit too fancy a word for the moves her body was able to perform. Fancy swaying might be more realistic.

She felt awkward trying to do anything more complicated than that, being all angles and long limbs, like a newborn foal, trying to stay upright. It wasn't her favourite thing to do and, quite frankly, she couldn't wait for this to be over.

Just keep smiling! Pretend you're having a great time.

Everyone else was having a great time. One or two had even paired off with a couple of guys who had bought them drinks. Thinking of which, she was beginning to get a little thirsty. She looked over at the bar, to see if there was much of a queue, and instead met a steady pair of beautiful blue eyes gazing back at her.

He was at the bar—the man in question. Holding a tall glass with what looked like water in it, condensation dripping down its sides. Black shirt, open at the collar. Black trousers.

She couldn't look away. She wanted to, but he held her

gaze, and somehow, before she knew it, he was standing in front of her.

'May I have this dance?'

The old-fashioned request was charming. If he'd said anything else, come out with a cheesy line, then she would have raised a sardonic eyebrow and turned away, but his question—polite, gallant, charming—hit all her buttons.

She could feel her cheeks flushing and was thankful he wouldn't be able to see that in the darkness. But the terrible thing about being in the dark was that it also made you throw a bit of caution to the wind. It created intimacy. And she couldn't help but laugh.

'You've seen me dance, right? The flailing?'

He smiled. 'It was utterly charming.'

'Charming?'

He leaned in. 'Adorable.'

And she liked him. He smelt great. She didn't know what it was, but she just felt secure with this guy. What was one more flail? They were in a public place. Nothing was going to *happen*.

'Sure. Okay.'

She bit her lip as he led her to the centre of the dance floor, and just as she was about to begin the music changed. It was almost as if this man and the DJ were in cahoots, because the music switched from a frantic, heated rhythm to something slow and soulful. The kind of music that begged couples to dance in each other's arms. Bodies pressed close. Intimate. Knowing.

She smiled and stepped shyly into his embrace, draping her arms over his shoulders as he pulled her to him.

He smelt delicious. Edible. A musky heat. And she closed her eyes as they swayed in tune together, sensing him inhale the scent of her shampoo as he lifted a tendril of her hair up to his nose. It was such an intimate gesture she felt shivers tremble down her spine, and her breath hitched in her throat as she wondered what he'd do next.

But he was a perfect gentleman. His hands didn't wander and she found herself wondering about this man in her arms. Who was he? Where had he come from? What was his name?

Why was he so *hot*?

She let him have the next dance. And then the next. And when she had to sit down, to give her feet and ankles a rest from the vertiginous heels she had unwittingly chosen for that evening, he walked her over to a place to sit and helped her slip them off. He massaged her feet for her whilst she squirmed in delight on the banquette and thanked the heavens that she'd had a pedicure two days ago.

He looked at her and smiled. 'Are you ticklish?'

'A bit.'

'Then I'll be careful.'

She liked the way he held her feet firmly, determined not to tickle her, but to give her the maximum benefit of his strong, capable hands.

'You know your way around a woman's foot.' Leah cringed once the words were out.

But he didn't raise an eyebrow. 'I know my way around many parts of the female anatomy.'

She blushed. The foot massage already had her biting her lip, trying her hardest not to moan and groan in delight at what was happening to her flesh, and his words made her wonder what magic he could cause in other places, with other parts of his anatomy?

But the thought was fleeting and quick. That wasn't who she was, so she knew she didn't have to worry about that. But somehow they got talking and chatting, and his name was Ben. So simple. So wonderful. It suited him.

She discovered they liked a lot of the same things—old movies, reading and the exact same brand of salted caramel chocolates—and when he learnt how close she lived he offered to give her a piggyback home.

'A piggyback?' she asked in amused disbelief. They weren't kids.

'You can't dance in those shoes and you certainly can't walk in them. I'm amazed you didn't break an ankle just getting here.'

The idea of him walking her home thrilled her. She didn't want to part company with him yet. But she didn't want to do this alone. Just in case. He could be anyone.

Hannah offered to accompany them for safety. Her friend lived in the block opposite her own. As good as his word, Ben carried her all the way back, telling them jokes and making them laugh, paying attention to both women fairly, though it was clear his interest was in her. And when he gently set her down on her feet, her soles pressed against the chilly pavement, she impulsively offered him a coffee or a nightcap, not yet willing to say goodbye.

He'd smiled. 'Coffee would be nice.'

Hannah waved them both goodbye, giving Leah a big thumbs-up sign in secret, when Ben wasn't looking.

She smiled and fished her keys out of her bag.

What am I doing? I don't do this. I don't invite random guys back!

But another voice in her head said, *Go for it! When are you going to get another chance?*

So she made him coffee. And they sat together on the couch, drinking it until it was gone, and the tension in the room was palpable.

'I should go.' His voice was loaded with regret. 'It was lovely spending a few hours with you, but I have an early start in the morning.'

She nodded. 'Me, too.'

She wasn't kidding either. She started a new job tomorrow. Going to the club had been in celebration of that.

He stood up and she stood with him. They were so close! Millimetres apart. Leah gazed up at his face, his mouth, and then he pulled her gently towards him and lowered his face to hers.

The kiss was perfect. Gentle.

Soft.

And then...

And then it wasn't. And they couldn't remove their clothes fast enough.

The touch of a finger trailing the length of her spine in a sinuous, serpentine stroke was enough to jerk her from the depths of a wonderful sleep to the stark, shocking reality that she was waking up with someone else in her bed.

Dr Leah Hudson's eyes blinked open in an instant as recollections of the previous night poured in, and in a panic she grabbed the duvet to her chest and leapt from the bed, dragging the quilt around her naked body, stumbling over it as she turned to see the man she'd left behind in the bedsheets.

Ben. Handsome. Fit—even with bed hair and a shadow of early-morning stubble. The man who had known his way around the female anatomy very well indeed, as it turned out.

Her naked male companion had woken at her sudden movement, and now lay propped up on an elbow, smiling at her in an irritatingly charming and attractive way, the curls that only last evening had been perfectly tamed now wild and tangled. In no way did that diminish his appeal. Somehow it increased it. And he didn't make any move to cover himself up. Deliciously confident man that he was. And she couldn't stop her gaze from travelling down…down…

Red-faced, she looked up again.

She envied him his confidence in his body. Hers had always let her down.

Ignoring the pleasant tingling she could feel from their combined fun last night, she felt her cheeks flush with heat. What must she look like? She'd gone to the club with Hannah and the others in full-on partying mode— mascara, lipstick, *glittery eyeshadow*, for goodness' sake! And after meeting the Adonis who now lay luxuriantly upon her comfiest blue cotton bedsheets she had brought him back to her place with the promise of a coffee or a nightcap and they had fallen into bed together without her having time to remove any of the muck from her face!

Did she look like a panda?

This was not like her at all. She wasn't a woman who did this kind of thing—one-night stands. Not that there was anything wrong with it, if it suited the people involved. But she'd always imagined herself as the *going-steady* type, waiting before she'd allow anyone the intimacy of her bed. That might be boring to some, but it had suited her perfectly until last night. It had given her a standard to uphold so that she didn't make her life complicated. Not letting anyone in because, really, what was the point? Life was complicated all on its own.

Now *he* lay on her bedsheets. Still here. *The next morning!* He wasn't meant to have stayed.

'Didn't I say you had to go? Remember? Just after midnight?'

'You exhausted me. I must have fallen asleep.'

He seemed oblivious to the fact that she wanted him out of there. Gorgeous or not. Seemed content to stay in her bed.

Leah clutched the quilt even tighter and glanced at her alarm clock beside the bed. Seven thirty-two a.m. She had slept with a strange man for over six hours, and him lying there looking like a wonderful breakfast delicacy was *not* helping. She had a new job to get to. An important job. Lives that might need saving.

Thinking about it, she really ought not to have agreed to going to the club.

'Look, last night was great, but—'

'Don't say *but*. Nothing ever great happens after someone says *but*.'

She smiled. '*But* I'm going to take a shower, and when I get out of the shower I don't want to find you're still here. You need to...' her gaze travelled along his wonderful torso, eyeing the hunk of gorgeousness she'd allowed herself last night '...put some clothes on and leave. Is that understood? You get what I'm saying, right?'

He nodded and smiled. 'Seems a shame to end something so great.'

Embarrassingly delighted, she smiled back. 'Maybe so, but that's the way it's going to be.'

She saw his trousers and designer underwear discarded on the floor of her living room, exactly where she'd torn them from his body, and picked them up, threw them at him.

'Start with these.' She gave him a broad, embarrassed smile. "It was a pleasure knowing you.'

Leah opened the shower door and listened for any strange sounds. The flat sounded pleasingly empty, so with one towel wrapped around her body and another around her hair, she unlocked her bathroom door and stepped out, listening once again just to make sure.

All she could hear were outside noises—singing birds, the odd car driving by. Nothing internal.

Thank God he's gone!

What had she been thinking? To do such a thing! Sleep with a stranger! Was that the behaviour of an expectant mother? Okay, to be fair, *she* wasn't the one expecting *herself.* She had a surrogate. Sally. Who was pregnant with Leah's baby.

Perhaps that's why I did it? One last mad fling? And I did choose a very nice candidate!

She smiled to herself. She would never find a guy like that in real life. And even if she did he'd probably run a mile as soon as she explained she was going to have a baby in seven months.

Leah paused to look into her spare room before she passed it. It was still filled with boxes from her recent move here. She really ought to get a move on and get it sorted into some sort of nursery. There was a cot in there somewhere, still waiting to be unfurled from its flat pack.

She padded through to her bedroom and then stopped, surprised.

He's made the bed! Wow. Did I manage to find the only hot, sexy, neat-freak?

The pillows had been fluffed, the sheets and duvet straightened and smoothed. He'd even picked up the bed runner from the floor and put it back on. And what was that on her pillow?

She bent to pick up the small piece of paper. Unfolding it, she saw a telephone number and a short note.

We had fun. Call me.

Leah bit her lip and smiled. He liked her. Wanted to see her again! She picked up the phone and dialled.

'Hello?'

'Sally, it's me. You're never going to believe what I did last night. Or rather, *who.*'

She heard a gasp from the other end. 'Naughty girl! Do tell. You know I've got to live vicariously through your adventures for the next two trimesters.'

Leah sank onto the edge of her bed. 'His name was Ben and he…er…stayed over.'

'What? *Damn!* I knew I should have tried harder to get babysitters for these monsters. Then I could have met him. Come on. I need details. What was he like? Tall? Dark, Handsome?' She giggled. 'Girthy?'

Leah laughed. 'Yes, to all of those.'

'You lucky girl.'

'And he was also polite and charming and funny— *and* he made the bed before he left.'

'You let him leave? He sounds like a keeper.'

'He's left me his number.'

'So call him!'

'I can't do that! He's only just gone. I need to leave it for a bit, don't I? Act cool?'

'Darling, you don't *do* cool. Get your first day out of the way, then give him a ring. Have fun whilst you can. Make hay whilst the sun shines—isn't that what they say?'

'Who?'

'I don't know. Farmers?'

Leah laughed. 'I've got to get ready for work. I did miss you last night.'

'Clearly. Look, I've got to go—William's just tipped orange juice over his brother.'

'Okay. I'll call you soon. Take care.'

'Bye.'

She could just imagine Sally's small brood descending into chaos. They were good kids, really. And she would have one of her own soon. Her own child. Thanks to Sally.

A man like Ben would probably run a mile at the sound of a baby. It wouldn't bring the kind of sleepless nights *he'd* be interested in.

Regretfully, she screwed up the piece of paper and dropped it in the bin.

It was time to get ready for work.

The baby was screaming its head off.

If ever I needed to hear a healthy set of lungs...well, this kid's got them.

Ben Willoughby smiled patiently at the mother as she tried her best to calm her distraught child, but her soothing words had no effect.

Clearly the baby did not like a strange man looming over him to try and listen to his heartbeat. Ben sat back. He felt sure the baby was absolutely fine, but it would be nice to check.

The mother had brought in the child, terrified by a strange rash that had appeared on her son's legs, especially his knees and the tops of his feet. It was red and raw-looking.

Her son had no temperature. No signs of illness at all, in fact, and Ben was sure he knew exactly what the rash had been caused by. But he didn't want this mother to feel as if she had wasted his time, so he was trying to be thorough and give the boy a check-up. Check-ups never hurt anyone.

'We'll wait for him to pipe down. I might get a nurse to distract him with bubbles or something—just so I can listen to his chest when he's quiet.'

'What do you think it is? Is it meningitis?' The mother peered at him, frowning in concern.

He shook his head. 'No, it's nothing like that. He's about eight months old?'

She nodded.

'Just started crawling?'

Another nod.

'I think it's carpet burns.'

He'd had plenty of the damn things as a child himself, and occasionally still got them now, when he had to play uncle and get down on the floor and pretend to have a great time. If he was honest, he *did* have a good time, but there was no way he was going to admit it.

Everyone knew he wasn't fond of kids. They were noisy and messy and they sucked away at your time and energies. They definitely weren't for him, and they most certainly would not be in his future. He intended to have a life that was entirely dedicated to himself, even if that seemed selfish to everyone else.

Because he knew that he wasn't. He was the least selfish person he knew. He gave everything of himself to others. Always had. But now his life was his own and he wanted it to stay that way. He'd seen what happened when you let other people get involved and it wasn't pretty. He intended to steer away completely from messy relationships.

And that was how he'd always played things—until this morning. When he'd woken in Leah's bed, completely satisfied, feeling warm and cosy and comfortable—until she'd stood up and yanked the quilt off him, anyway. He could still picture it. How embarrassed she'd looked. The charming flush that had bloomed in her cheeks. Her twinkling eyes. The way she'd thrown his clothes at him before she'd shuffled out of the room in her quilt cocoon.

Delightful.

And he wasn't sure just what it was, but before he had left he had felt compelled to leave his number.

I never leave my number. I never ask for more.

He'd closed the door to her flat after fighting the strong temptation to join her in the shower and then stood there for a moment, unable to get back in, wondering if he'd made a mistake. Why break the habit of a lifetime?

He supposed he could screen his calls, but a part of him didn't want to. And it wasn't the part below his belt, strangely enough. It was in his head. He wanted to know more about the delicious minx he'd run into last night. More about the woman who'd made him smile with her own smile. Who'd made him feel amazed by her laughter. Whose capacity for dancing was equal to that of a newborn giraffe on rollerblades. Who'd awoken something within him that he'd never felt before...

'Carpet burns? You're sure?'

'Absolutely.' He pulled up the scrubs on his left leg to show her the carpet burns he had from being made to be a horse by his four-year-old niece Gemma. 'I've got matching ones. But we'll give him a proper check-over once he's quiet.'

The mother blushed. 'Oh, I feel so stupid.'

He smiled. 'Don't be. You're entitled to worry about your baby.'

'But I've wasted your time!'

'No, you haven't. It's always important to get something checked if it concerns you. What if it had been something serious and you'd dismissed it? We'd rather it be a false alarm than something serious. Wouldn't we?'

He gave another of his winning smiles, hoping the screaming child would soon be quiet, and the mother smiled back, thanking him.

'I'll be back in a few minutes.'

He left the cubicle, intending to fill in a chart or two and give the boy time to get his breath back, then glanced up to see how the waiting room was filling up.

And there she was.

The woman from last night, walking towards him in a floaty white blouse and a pencil-slim skirt that hugged in all the right places.

Leah.

She stopped upon seeing him.

He watched in delight as her cheeks flushed once again, and he knew that that was something he would never tire of seeing.

But why was she *here*? Was she hurt? Or had she known somehow where he worked and come to throw his telephone number back in his face?

'Hi,' he said, somewhat lost for words.

He never usually had this. The morning after. That awkward conversation. The embarrassed excuses. He got the good part—the flirting, the excitement, the kissing, the hot sex. He never had to worry about the *afterwards* because there never was one.

She looked like a startled deer. He saw her swallow.

'Wh…what are *you* doing here?'

CHAPTER TWO

OH, MY GOD. You idiot! He's wearing scrubs and has a stethoscope around his neck. What do you think *he's doing here?*

She felt her cheeks colour again and sucked in a deep, steadying breath.

Okay, think. He's obviously a doctor here, but maybe he's from another department and he's only down here providing a consult...

Because it would be mortifying to have to work closely with the guy she'd met in a club and slept with last night. A guy she'd kicked out of her flat because he'd over-stayed his welcome.

Oh, dear. What must he think of me?

But then a bit of courage pushed its way forward and reminded her that what she'd done last night had not been done alone. He'd done it, too. So what did *she* think of him?

Her brain provided her with a helpful reminder of what he'd looked like naked on her bed after she'd swooped up with the quilt.

Blushing—*again!*—she managed a smile. 'I say stupid things sometimes. Clearly you're a doctor, here. Obviously...'

He smiled back and it did strange things to her insides.

The way he was looking at her…as if she were edible and he wanted to gobble her up!

'I am. You're right.'

'A…um…registrar? Consultant? From… I don't know. Maybe Orthopaedics, or something?' she asked hopefully.

'Consultant. Emergency medicine.'

'Oh.'

She looked about her, panicking slightly. He worked *here*? In this department? That wasn't good. Oh, no, that wasn't good at all!

'May I ask why *you're* here?' He grinned his cheeky chappie smile and then leaned in to whisper, 'Physically you seem to be in full working order, so…?'

She laughed. Almost hysterically. Then stopped. What to say? She could lie and say she was here visiting someone? Or maybe she could say…?

No other lies popped into her head. She was stuck with telling the truth. Because she had to. The 'visiting someone' lie wouldn't help, would it? She had a job to do here. She needed the money and she'd been hoping for the possibility of the position becoming permanent.

'I've…um…come here to work.'

She smiled quickly, alarmingly, then continued before he could say anything.

'I start today. Here. In this department. As a…locum.'

She saw the dawning realisation on his face and was glad to see that he was somewhat taken aback too. That was good. It was nice to feel that they were on even footing.

He laughed. '*You're* my new doctor?'

She matched his laugh. 'That's me!'

Leah watched him take this in—watched as an interesting fleet of emotions passed over his face—and felt her own heart beat faster as she realised just how much she would be working with this man over the next few months. Her one-night stand. Her *boss*.

Had she screwed up? Already? Or would he be the decent guy she hoped he was and let them start with a fresh new page?

That was possible, right? To pretend as if nothing had happened when in reality you knew more about a man than you should and exactly what touch would make him gasp with delight and ecstasy? They'd be able to work together as if they'd never met before.

Right?

Right?

Molly, one of the nurses, was asked to show her around as Ben had got called in to Majors. A trauma was coming in via helicopter.

Molly was about the same age as her, and was bright, friendly and chatty. She took her around Minors, showing her where everything was, who to ask for help, and what the password was for the computer system, and then she took her into Majors.

Leah couldn't help but look at Ben as he assessed his new patient, strapped to a backboard that was being brought in by the helicopter medics. He was more than just handsome. He was breathtaking. No wonder he had caught her eye in the club last night. Broad-shouldered, flat stomach, trim waist...

And I know all the other details, too...

The tiny mole just above his left hipbone. The smoothness of his skin. The toned musculature of that inverted V below the hipbones that led down to his...

Molly must have caught her staring, because she chuckled. 'Ah, yes, you've noticed Mr Willoughby. I don't blame you. We all think he's gorgeous! Just beware, though, you don't fall for his charms.'

Leah blinked. 'What? Oh, no, I wouldn't. I—'

'He's gone out on dates with quite a few members of staff and he likes to play the field, if you know what I mean? Not that I want to talk badly about someone I work with—he's a really nice guy, actually—but he's quite the heartbreaker.'

Molly was talking to her in that *all-girls-together-against-men* way, so Leah played along.

'I understand perfectly.' She nodded as if she were a wise old woman. But for some strange reason it hurt to think that she was one in a long line of conquests. She'd hoped that because she'd indulged in once-in-a-lifetime behaviour maybe he had, too.

How many others had he slept with? He was a Lothario and she'd fallen for his charms and given him everything. It was the oldest trick in the book. Knowing that made her feel even more glum that her hot one-night stand was definitely not going to settle for a woman who was about to become a mother, no matter how hot the sex with her had been!

She resigned herself to seeing no more of that kind of action with him. They'd had one night and one night it would stay—never to be repeated. She was just a notch on his bedpost and she would not pine after him, despite how he had made her feel. She had a future ahead of her. It was never going to be with him. It was a good thing that she had thrown away his telephone number.

'What else is there to see?' Leah walked away from the trauma, wanting to move on from Ben. To stop staring at him as if she was hypnotised. In more ways than one.

She felt foolish for thinking that there'd been more to her one-night stand. That her night with Ben, even though a one-off, had somehow had more meaning to it than any one-night stand other people might have. That theirs had been different. That it hadn't just been a tacky get-together so that both people could scratch an itch.

But apparently it had. Sleeping with a woman for one night was normal behaviour for him, it seemed, and she was just one more in a long line of women who'd probably thought for a brief moment that they were special.

It had felt good to feel special. She'd never really had that. Had never been wanted. So it had felt good to let herself believe that maybe she did have something that he wanted. She did have value.

But it had just been sex. All he'd wanted was release. It hadn't been *her* in particular. Any woman would have done.

And he'd used her—the way he probably used all women.

Even if he *had* made the bed for her afterwards.

Leah felt a little sick, but it was a feeling she was used to. The realisation that she wasn't special.

She never had been. Not in her entire life. She'd had to make her own happiness.

I should be used to it.

Which was why she had a surrogate. Leah had always wanted a family and, knowing she couldn't get one the normal way, by having one herself, she had decided to take matters into her own hands and find her own happiness.

She could only ever rely on herself not to let her down.

Because anyone she had allowed to get close had *always* let her down.

The thought of having to rely on a surrogate had seemed an almost impossible task. How could she not suspect that the surrogate would change her mind? That she'd want to keep the baby for herself? She'd got her mind so twisted on all the things that could go wrong she'd even considered not doing it!

Until Sally had offered. Her best friend Sally. Who already had three children of her own. Whose family was already complete. Sally had loved her enough to offer to do this.

So, okay, maybe she had one person in her corner.

And when the baby was born Leah would have two. Sally and the baby. And the baby would be her own flesh and blood. From *her* egg. Used after months of injections and hormones to help her ovaries produce an egg that was in a healthy enough condition to use.

It had been important that the baby was her own. Because she'd never had a family. No mum or dad. No siblings. No friendly aunts or uncles or grandparents.

Leah had had the care system. And it had been horrible. And her yearning for a family had become so strong since she'd become an adult and started working in medicine.

Seeing what other people had.

Seeing what *she* could have if she were brave enough to try.

And now she would be a mother soon.

And she was going to let no one, most especially not Mr Ben Willoughby, ruin that for her.

Ben peered closer at the X-ray. There were clear fractures of the distal end of the ulna and radius. Thankfully they weren't displaced. The motorcyclist had put his arms out to break his fall when he'd come off his bike. He'd need to get an orthopaedic consult to make sure what treatment was needed. Most probably an open reduction and internal fixation with plates and screws.

He was just about to pick up the phone to call Orthopaedics when Leah came to sit beside him.

'Hi.'

He turned to look at her with a smile. It had been a pleasant surprise to learn that she was his new locum, and if he was honest about it he was quite pleased. He'd wanted to hear from her again and get to know her a bit more, and now that she was here for the next few months he'd get that chance.

Which is a first for me...

He gazed at her more intently, trying to work out why this woman intrigued him. Apart from the obvious gorgeousness that she didn't seem to know she had. Perhaps it was that smiley persona? Perhaps it was the way she could blush so innocently and yet also be a siren in bed? That clash and juxtaposition of opposites was completely messing with his head.

Maybe it was her eyes? They twinkled and shone with a brightness he'd never noticed before in a woman. Maybe it was the way she couldn't hide what she was feeling—everything was written there for him to see on her face.

And, looking at her now, he could sense she had something to tell him. She was biting her lower lip. Out of anxiety, clearly, but all it did was pull his focus to her mouth, her full lips, and he felt a physical yearning to reach out and brush his thumb over her lower lip, to free it, and then pull her face towards his and...

'I need to talk to you.'

Oh. Conversations like this never end well.

And the reason he knew that was because it was usually *him* saying stuff like that. Trying to tell some woman he'd dated for one night to stop calling him. That he wasn't interested. That she really ought to start looking elsewhere because he wouldn't be going out with her again. He always tried to be nice about it, though. Polite. Kind.

Was she really going to do that to him? When they'd had something so *good*?

'I think I know what you're going to say.'

She looked at him, her brows furrowed. Confused. 'You do?'

He nodded. 'I do. You're going to say something along the lines of, *Look, we're colleagues...we really shouldn't be going out with each other...can we just be friends?* Am I right?'

She bit her lip again.

He really wished she wouldn't do that. It was down-right distracting. Wonderfully so.

'Well, yes...kind of.'

He turned to face her, making sure there was no one else in earshot. 'I think you're wrong.'

She blushed, and he felt his insides go funny again.

'I'm not wrong. You wouldn't be interested in me. Not at all. Not if you knew the truth...' She trailed off, clearly trying to find the right words to explain whatever predicament she thought she was in.

'Are you married?' He didn't think she was. There'd been no sign of someone living with her in that flat of hers.

'No.'

'Do you have a steady boyfriend?'

She looked about, also checking there was no one else listening in to their conversation. 'No.'

'Then what's the problem? You've got to see this from my point of view. Boy meets girl...boy goes back to girl's apartment and they have a great time. Boy knows this. Girl knows this. It makes sense that they do it again to see how great they can really make it.'

He grinned, feeling all sorts of things firing inside his belly at the thought of another night with this woman. And not just his belly. Being this close to her, almost touching her, inhaling that gentle perfume of hers…it was *intoxicating*! Surely she wasn't going to throw this opportunity away? They could have fun for a bit…

She was staring deeply into his eyes, almost as if she were looking into his soul, and then suddenly she blinked and sat back, moving away from him. She glanced nervously around them, before scooching closer again on her chair.

'I had a great time with you, yes. Of course it was…' She blushed. 'Hot. But I'm not the kind of woman you would want to get involved with right now.'

'You're wrong—'

'I'm going to have a baby.'

He sat up straight and looked at her, the smile gone from his face.

A baby? *What?* He looked down at her abdomen, trying to think back to how she'd looked, naked in the moonlight streaming in through her open curtains. The soft swell of her abdomen…her wondrous curves…

'No, not me. Not me in person. I have a surrogate. My best friend Sally—she's carrying my baby for me and she's got seven more months before she gives birth.'

He stared. Shocked beyond words. He'd found the perfect woman. At least he thought he had.

This changes everything!

She was going to have a baby. She was going to become a mother. Which was great for her, but not for him. He didn't need that kind of complication in his life. Parenthood? Responsibilities? Resentment? Exhaustion?

No, thanks. No way, José.

CHAPTER THREE

'YOU'RE SHOCKED. I know you're shocked. I would be, too, if I were in your shoes.'

She smiled a little, to show him she understood. That she wasn't going to blame him if he walked away now. In fact she *needed* him to walk away. Because he was a complication that she didn't need in her life right now. A stunningly attractive complication, yes, but not the kind she would be able to rely on with a baby around. He'd hardly signed up for this, after all. It was only right he knew from the start, so he could make decisions with all the facts at his fingertips.

He could cause wonders with those fingertips... Don't think about those. Focus!

'A baby? You're going to be a mum?'

'Yes. I am.'

'But...isn't surrogacy like a last chance kind of thing?'

She could see what he wanted to ask. *Why can't you have the child yourself?* Perhaps she needed to explain? But this felt awkward. She barely knew him, after all. Carnal knowledge of a person didn't count in this situation. She wasn't used to sharing personal information with someone she hardly knew. But it had to be done.

'It *is* a last chance kind of thing.'

'But why? You're only in your thirties, I'm guessing. You still might meet someone.'

'I appreciate your optimism—I do. But it's not that simple.'

'I don't understand. What aren't you telling me?'

Boy, those eyes of his are intense!

She sucked in a deep breath. *Here goes.*

'I've been told that I probably can't carry a baby to term due to an anomaly in my uterus, but I want to start a family and this seemed the safest way to do that.'

Ben frowned, a small divot forming between his brows. 'What kind of anomaly?'

'A bicornuate uterus.'

He sucked in a breath. 'It's partially split?'

He was a good listener. It made him easy to tell.

'Mine's quite severe. My doctors told me that any baby I carry would most likely be lost in the second trimester, or that there'd be foetal growth retardation—especially if the foetus implanted in one of the two halves.'

He nodded. 'I've heard of it. But I've never met anyone with it before.'

'That you know of.'

He smiled. 'You're my first.'

She nodded, smiling. 'Yes, well. There you go. Intimacy *and* a medical revelation. Aren't you a lucky guy?'

He nodded.

'I've never had family,' she said. 'I want to belong to someone. I want someone who is my blood. Someone to love and cherish, who cherishes me in return. I always knew I wanted a child and I just felt that time was running out for me to find that with someone I could trust enough.'

He looked doubtful. 'So you're doing it on your own?'

She smiled, glad that he understood and didn't appear to be judging her. 'So I'm doing it on my own.'

He didn't need to hear about the long months of needles and hormones and egg collection procedures. She'd had one hot night with this man—she didn't want him to think of her lying back in a room with her legs in stirrups. She didn't want him thinking of her as a patient. Those days, she hoped, were over. The future was going to be everything.

'Which is why you needed to know.'

'And you think I won't be interested in you because you're about to become a parent?'

Leah cocked her head to one side, smiling. 'Well? Are you?'

He leaned back in his chair, considering his answer. 'You think I'll run a mile because a baby is on the way?'

She laughed. 'Yes.'

He held his chest as if she'd just stabbed him in the heart and mock-groaned. 'I'm hurt!'

'Come on! Are you seriously trying to tell me that a man like you isn't put off by a woman like me?'

His eyes twinkled. *'"A man like me"?'*

Clearly he wanted clarification.

'You have a reputation, Mr Willoughby. As a bit of a player.'

He shook his head, smiling, as if he were disappointed in her. 'You've been here one morning and already you're listening to gossip?'

She maintained eye contact. 'You still haven't answered my question.'

He stared back, giving a half-smile, considering how to answer.

She knew the answer in her heart. And it was a shame, because she really had had a great night with him. And it hadn't been just the sex, but all the talking they'd done beforehand. The laughing. The enjoyment of his company. The great foot massage! There'd been something there. Something not acknowledged by either of them. A spark. A connection. A flame.

But she never got his answer. An alarm sounded from Majors. A cardiac arrest. So they both leapt from their seats and made a mad dash towards the noise.

Answers would have to wait.

The next two weeks were difficult and awkward. Ben wasn't sure how to be around Leah. He liked her. *Really* liked her. She was funny and smart and everyone in the department loved her. She had such a friendly manner people would confide in her, talk to her. And her laugh… Whenever he heard it, he felt as if it was warming his soul. He wanted to be pulled into her orbit. He did. But he kept holding back.

She was going to become a mother soon. And he wanted to be happy for her, but he couldn't help but feel that she'd rushed this decision. All that stuff she'd said about wanting a family, feeling that bond and having someone who loved her… It was an idealised view of what family could be. She was looking at life through rose-tinted spectacles. People—families—they didn't all live in Happy Land, where everyone got on and loved one another. There could be discord and hatred and resentment. Being someone's blood relative didn't guarantee you happiness. Didn't guarantee you a free pass in life to joy.

Families were hard work. His own had been. And families could rip your heart out.

Leah probably thought that having a baby would mean everything to her—and maybe it would to begin with.

But had she thought about sleepless nights and tantrums? Problems at school?

His younger brother and sister had run the whole gamut. In their early teens they'd hated him and rebelled against him. They would stay out all night with friends in lonely parks whilst he stayed at home. Worrying about them. Often having to head out to try and find them.

Families equalled stress, and there would be so many moments when she would want to run away but would feel unable to. Because of her responsibility.

But how could he tell her any of that? How could he squash her dream, knowing how much it meant to her?

He was pondering this problem as he went to see his first patient of the day. He was working in Minors today, and he held a triage form that stated his next patient had been hurt during a bout of shoplifting.

He shook his head in disbelief. Shoplifting!

Ben pulled back the curtain and there on the bed sat a teenage girl, probably no older than fifteen or so, and across from her a burly-looking security guard.

'Miss Tammy Fields?'

The girl glowered at the guard. 'Yeah.'

He pulled the curtain around them for some privacy. Tammy sat on the bed, one leg on a pillow. He could see her ankle looked a little swollen.

'You've hurt your left foot? How did that happen?'

'*He* did it!'

'I did not—' the security guard began, bristling.

'How else did I end up on the floor? You tripped me!'

'You were stealing!'

'Wait a minute!' Ben held up his hands for quiet. 'You're not her parent?'

'No, thank goodness. If she were mine, I'd—'

'Then why don't you wait outside? I'll come and talk to you in a moment.'

'I'm not taking my eyes off her. She'll make a run for it.'

'With this ankle? I highly doubt it. Now, please...' He held the curtain open so the security guard could pass through, albeit reluctantly. 'If you wait in the waiting room, I'll be through to see you soon.'

The guard disappeared, with one last look over his shoulder that seemed to say, *If you run...*

Ben sighed with relief when he'd gone, then sank back onto his stool and looked at the young girl. 'Tell me what happened.'

'I was getting some food—tinned stuff. Only I didn't have enough money for all of it and I thought they wouldn't miss it. It was a pound shop! It means nothing to them! And we're starving...'

'We?'

'Me and my brothers. Only they're really little so I left 'em at home.'

'So you *were* shoplifting?'

'To feed the kids! I *had* to. I had no other choice!'

He frowned, taking in her slightly neglected appearance. 'Where are your parents?'

'Mum's away.'

'At work?'

Tammy laughed. 'Yeah, *right*. She's at her boyfriend's house. She does this. Goes away for a few days and leaves us to get on with things. Only there's never no food in the house and she don't leave us no money. And the little ones are hungry, so I... I took stuff.'

'How did you hurt your ankle?'

'That big idiot tripped me and I dropped the cans.

One went under my foot or something. My ankle hurt after that.'

'He brought you in?'

'Yeah.'

'Who's with your brothers?'

She looked down and away. 'No one. I had to do this. I *had* to!' she cried, finally realising the implications of her situation.

He would have to call Social Care. Report this. And then this family would spend months with interference from professionals to make sure they had support and that the mother stopped abandoning her children. Only Social Services could help them make this better.

He smiled at the young girl and passed her a tissue from a box. 'Can I take a look at your ankle?'

She wiped her nose and sniffed. 'Sure.'

He gave her ankle and foot a cursory examination, checking for range of movement, whether she had sensation, whether she could wriggle her toes. It didn't seem broken—probably more of a bad sprain. But they'd need an X-ray, just to confirm, because she had some swelling there already.

'I'm going to send you to X-Ray.'

'You think it's broken?'

'No. But we need to be on the safe side.'

'Oh, *man*! Mum's going to kill me.'

'I also need her number. To inform her that you're here.'

'She won't come.'

'Even so…'

Reluctantly, Tiffany gave him her mother's mobile number. 'Don't tell her I was shoplifting.'

'She'll find out. I'm sure that security guard will let her know.'

'Well, let's hope she's too drunk to take it all in.'

Leah slipped into the morning handover, hoping nobody would notice that she was a good ten minutes late. It wasn't her fault. She'd been on her way in to work, perfectly on time, when a giant seagull had let rip from above, splattering the front of her jacket. There'd been no way she could turn up at work looking like that, and the one solitary tissue she'd had in her pocket had not been enough. So back home she'd gone, to swap jackets and put the dirtied one in the laundry.

She'd heard that having a bird poop on you was meant to be good luck, but she really couldn't see how that worked. Just because it was a rare occurrence, it didn't mean that she was going to be more likely to win the lottery, did it?

What it had made her was late for work...

She closed the door quietly behind her and slipped into the nearest available chair. She placed her bag on the floor and beamed a smile at the person closest to her—and then looked up, only to see that Ben was sitting directly opposite her.

'Nice of you to join us, Dr Hudson.'

All eyes turned to her and she coloured under the onslaught. 'Er...thank you. Sorry I'm late. There was a poop incident...'

Her voice trailed off as she realised that maybe not everyone would want to hear about that. Or, God forbid, thought *she* was the one with the dodgy bowels!

'It was a seagull. It wasn't me! I...er...' As everyone began to smile at her, she flushed and made a zipping motion over her mouth.

Best be quiet, I think...

'Dr Evers, if you'd like to continue?' Ben spoke to the doctor who had been in charge of last night's shift.

Leah politely accepted the handover sheet passed to her by the doctor to her right as Dr Evers filled them in on what had happened last night and who they still had in bays in Resus, Majors and Minors.

As always it had been busy—a mix of falls, chest pain, broken bones, and one patient with rhabdomyolisis, a condition in which muscle broke down rapidly. He was being treated with isotonic saline to deal with the swelling of the muscle tissue and to prevent damage to his kidneys and was currently resting, awaiting transfer to a ward.

She glanced at Ben, appreciating the chance to be able to look at him without being observed.

He'd been perfectly nice to her over the last couple of weeks. He'd even asked her if she wanted to go on a trip the department had organised. That had surprised her...

'If you're not working on the fifteenth, a group of us are going to Finley Towers—the amusement park. Want to come?' he'd asked.

'Are you asking me out on a date?'

'Well, it's a group thing, so... Anyway, if you're free. Thought it might be fun for you. You know—before the shackles of parenthood weigh you down.'

She'd smiled at the time, but his comment had left her wondering. There had just been something a little off with him, ever since she'd told him about Sally and the surrogacy.

He was keeping her at arm's length—pretty much as she'd suspected he would—but just because she'd expected him to do it, it didn't mean it was any less disappointing and upsetting. They'd had a closeness. An intimacy. And now there were barriers.

They'd spent a night together and, yes, it had been only a one-night stand, but they'd had a rare connection. At least she'd thought so! Or perhaps she was behind the times and this was how people behaved nowadays? But she did feel he was letting her down.

What did I even want from him? He's my boss—it would never work.

But knowing it didn't make it any easier. It was just another example of people failing her expectations. And she was used to that. Having to stand alone. Why should it be any different with him?

He was just a guy who'd discovered his one-night stand had complications in her life—why would he want to be a part of that?

She sighed, and it must have been louder than she realised, because once again all eyes were on her. 'Sorry. I didn't mean…' Her cheeks flushed. 'Carry on.'

She looked down at the table and scribbled something on her piece of paper that she hoped made it look as if she was concentrating. Which she wasn't. Which was bad.

Why couldn't she get him out of her head? She was always thinking about him. Looking for him. Each day she came in and checked the roster, and she felt her heart sink if he wasn't on the same shift as her. And yesterday she'd been coming out of a cubicle at the exact same time as he came out of the one opposite and their eyes had met and they'd smiled and…

Nothing. He'd given her a slight nod, an acknowledgement, but that was all, and after he'd walked away she'd felt…deflated. Yep. That was the word, all right!

He'd made it perfectly clear that he wasn't interested.

So why did he ask if I'd go to Finley Towers? It sounded like he wanted me to go.

And she did want to go. It would be fun. She wasn't rostered that day and neither was he.

Not that I checked or anything...

Perhaps it would be a chance to spend some time with him away from the hospital? Where they would get a chance to talk? Not many people got the opportunity to get to know a one-night stand better and she really wanted them to be different. She hoped he would be a good friend, if nothing else. They had to make *something* good out of this.

Leah glanced up at him and met his gaze.

He was looking at her with a hunger she recognised, but as soon as he realised she'd caught him looking he quickly glanced away. He looked awkward for a moment, and then he shifted in his seat. He began to nibble on the end of his pen.

Had he been thinking of their night together?

She wouldn't blame him. Because she did it, too.

He was a difficult man to forget.

CHAPTER FOUR

As soon as the handover had finished Ben was out of his chair and on his way out through the door. It was getting increasingly difficult for him to spend time with Leah, simply because of the way his thoughts kept running. And a small part of him was hoping that she wouldn't make it to the work outing at Finley Towers, because if she did he'd have to spend time with her and it wouldn't be work. It would be laughter and fun and friendship, and he might see yet another side of her that he really liked, and...

She's beautiful. I love the way she blushes when she's embarrassed. I love it when she smiles.

His thoughts were running away with themselves, as if he were some young teenage boy with a crush, idolising her, putting her on some kind of pedestal. He was hungry for every glimpse he could get of her, eager for every word she spoke, yearning to spend some more intimate time with her once again.

Where was it all coming from?

He hadn't been on a second date with anyone for years, and the one he had gone on before that had been disastrous. He'd liked the woman—of course he had—but something just hadn't been there the second time. The spark had gone. The thrill of being with someone new hadn't been there and he'd gone home early.

Why did he suspect it would be very different with Leah?

Anyway he'd asked her if she was free to go on the department outing to Finley Towers, the amusement park. It had the UK's highest, fastest rollercoaster and there was nothing he loved more than a rollercoaster.

A group trip would be fine, wouldn't it? Safer. Less pressure on them to be alone together. And he would be able to see what she was like away from the hospital.

And out of bed!

Not that bed hadn't been amazing. It had. It was just that he knew there was *more* with someone like Leah.

Someone like Leah... Of course there's more. She's going to be a mother.

That bothered him more than he cared to admit. He'd seen so many people lose who they were when they became parents. They forgot their own loves, their own passions, because they were so busy being Mum or Dad. Days became all about mealtimes and nappy changes and bedtime routines, and the people they'd been before becoming parents disappeared in all that care and concern and worry.

Where would Leah go?

How long would it take for her to disappear beneath the avalanche of baby care?

Irritated by the thought, he picked up his first patient file and saw that it was for a child with a cut above his eyebrow. Frowning, he went to the cubicle, and as he got closer could hear a cacophony of noise that only a large amount of children could produce. There was crying and tears, the urgent low voice of a parent trying to calm everyone down, and mischievous rebellion of children ignoring her urgings.

I'm not going to tolerate that noise whilst I'm working!

He yanked the curtain back, hoping that the sudden movement would make everyone pipe down, but he was barely noticed.

A mother sat on the edge of the bed, cradling one child to her, holding a tea towel against his head, whilst another child jumped on the bed, a smaller toddler rammed his toy car repeatedly into the wall and another sat in the chair, holding a book that had the ability to make irritating musical sounds at the press of a button.

'Alfie Cotton?' he asked.

The mother looked up, her face breaking into relief at the sight of him, a doctor. 'Yes! Thank you! He's got quite a large cut above his left eyebrow.'

Ben grabbed a pair of gloves from the dispenser on the wall and then got the mother to lower the tea towel for him to have a proper look. It wasn't that big—maybe a centimetre—but it was enough to have caused what looked like a lot of blood loss. Head wounds were notorious for bleeding a lot.

'How did it happen?'

'He was bouncing on the bed and he fell off and hit the radiator on the wall. I told him not to do it! But they never listen.'

Considering there was a child on the bed behind her, also bouncing around, he could see quite clearly that they didn't listen. Why had she brought them all with her to A&E? Perhaps she had no one she could trust to babysit?

Never mind, he'd have to get on with it. He needed to check the wound properly, to see whether it needed gluing or stitches, but first he'd have to clean it.

As he leaned forward for another look little Alfie

screamed a protest and tried to slither from his mother's arms.

'Alfie, no! Sit still!' His mother tried to hoist him back up.

Ben could tell this was going to be difficult. Perhaps he'd need those bubbles again?

'I'll just go and get what I need and then we'll see what we can do, all right?'

He closed the curtain behind him and went to the room where all their equipment was laid out on trays stacked from ceiling to floor. He could get everything in here—plasters, tweezers, Vicryl acrylic for stitching, saline wash. All that he needed to help soothe or cure all manner of ills and injuries.

He let out a heavy sigh.

'Hey.'

It was Leah. She stood in the doorway and smiled at him and he could have sworn his heart almost skipped a beat.

'Hi.'

'You look tense.'

'I *am* tense.'

'Oh, dear. The shift's only just started. Need a hand with anything? Or anyone?'

'Don't you have a patient of your own?'

'Just gone to X-Ray. Suspected fracture of the clavicle. Came off his bike and hit a railing. You?'

'Child with a head wound. Only the mum has had to bring the entire brood and it's like working in a nursery. Kids everywhere.'

She smiled. 'I'm used to that. Do they bother you? Kids? I kind of get the feeling you're not their biggest fan.'

'Whatever gave that away?' He raised an eyebrow and laughed.

She smiled at him. 'Just some of the things that you say.'

'I'm the oldest of three. I've done my fair share of hanging around with toddlers.'

'Three kids? Your mum and dad must have loved having babies.'

He grabbed the glue. She had no idea what it had been like for him at home.

'Having them—maybe. Looking after them? That was a different story.'

Now she frowned. 'Do you want to talk about it?'

He *never* wanted to talk about it. Which was why the urge to tell her everything felt strange. He *wanted* her to know. Felt that she would sit and listen to him if he blurted it all out. The whole sorry mess. All he'd had to do.

He had to fight the urge to let it all come out of him, even though he knew Leah would understand. But it wasn't right to burden her with all that. Although she'd shared a secret with him… It would balance them out, right?

Ben hesitated, torn between wanting to tell her everything and keeping it all to himself. As he always had done. His fear won out.

'I'm okay. Though are you any good at blowing bubbles?'

'Erm…yes…'

'Good.' He handed her a pot that came with a wand. 'You can be my distraction technique. Follow me.'

He headed back to the cubicle, acutely aware of her following behind him. He introduced Leah to the flustered mum and explained what they were about to do.

'I'm going to use glue to close the wound. It's got nice straight edges, and it's not bleeding any more, so it should come together quite nicely.'

The mum nodded.

'We'll do it with him sitting on your lap, as he seems comfortable there. Dr Hudson will try to distract him with bubbles as it might sting just a little when I put the glue on, so hold him quite firmly.'

'Okay...'

Leah began blowing when Ben was ready to seal the wound and, as expected, little Alfie became mesmerised by the little bubbles floating in front of his face, reaching out to touch them and even blowing some of his own as Ben painted the glue onto the edges of the wound and applied small sterile strips to cover it afterwards.

'There. All done.'

The mother laughed. 'He didn't even notice!'

'The power of soapy water.'

Ben cleared away his equipment.

'Try and keep the wound dry for about five days and don't let him scratch or pick at it. If it becomes red or swollen he'll need to see a doctor—but you can go to your GP for that.'

'Thank you, Doctor.'

'My pleasure. You can take them all home again now.'

'Thanks.'

They started to pack up all their belongings and he left the cubicle with Leah, who'd handed over the bubbles to Alfie to keep.

He sat down at the doctor's desk to write up his notes. 'Thanks for helping out.'

'No problem at all.'

He looked at her. At how relaxed she was. 'Kids seem to like you.'

'I like kids.'

'It shows.' He began writing on Alfie's patient file. She tilted her head to one side. 'But you don't.'

It wasn't a question. Clearly. And the statement made him feel uncomfortable.

People were meant to like kids, weren't they? To be genetically predisposed to carry on the human race? That was the whole point to the continuation of the species. Kids were meant to be cute and wonderful, funny and lovable. What did it say about him that kids made him want to run away?

He sighed. 'I don't *hate* kids, *per se.*'

'But?'

'But… I didn't have the greatest of childhoods, and neither did my brother and sister. Perhaps it's not kids that I don't like…just bad parents.'

She was silent for a moment whilst she digested that nugget he'd just provided.

He felt his cheeks colour at the intensity of her concentration and put down his pen and shrugged, knowing he had to explain. 'I had to grow up really fast. Ten years old and I had to look after two younger kids whilst my parents slept or drank or got stoned. I had to cook for them, and clean up after them, and care for them when they got sick. My parents might have known how to *make* babies, but they sure screwed up at taking care of us.'

He continued to write Alfie's notes with a determination he'd never felt before, stopping only when Leah laid her hand upon his to still it.

He stared at her hand, his heart pounding in his chest like a jackhammer, his stomach swirling like a whirlpool.

'I'm sorry you had it tough. It shouldn't have been like that for you.'

'Yeah, well… I got over it.'

'Did you?'

He looked away from the intensity in her eyes. How could she see right into his very soul? He worked so hard to keep that part of his history hidden and—what?—one glance from her and he let it all spill out? What *was* that? Why had it happened?

'I just don't understand how you want to be a parent so badly. I've never wanted kids of my own. I could never saddle myself like that again.'

She said nothing, and he wasn't sure whether he ought to look at her face and see what she was thinking. Was she astounded by what he'd said? Upset? Angry? Or was she sympathetic?

'Not every parent is awful. Some of them care. A lot of them do. They idolise their children. Adore them. That's what I intend to do. That's who I'm going to be. One of those parents who gives her child everything.'

He looked up at her. Met her gaze.

She was smiling at him, and he was happy about that. Leah's smiles were wondrous things. They made him feel better about everything. Made him feel happy within himself. He could feel himself conceding the argument.

'Then your baby is going to be very lucky indeed.'

'Thanks. You don't think that one day you might be able to think that way, too? Put right a wrong? Make a child your world?'

No. He helped children through his work. That was enough. Because that didn't hurt—there was professional distance. Have a child of his own? That was too much to contemplate. He never wanted to be a father. *Never.*

He shook his head.

'That's a shame. I think you'd make a great dad. I bet your brother and sister think so, too.'

They did think that. Were grateful for all he had done. They often asked him why he didn't have kids of his own yet and he always laughed it off. They didn't know that he was serious. He was the only one who didn't. All those nieces and nephews…

He was happy for them. Happy that despite their shared experience of childhood they'd grown up to go on and have their own babies and become parents.

But it was different for him. He'd been the one with the responsibility. He'd been the one with the worries and the concerns and the sleepless nights. Not them. They'd looked up to him. They'd never known what it was like to be a young parent.

Because that was what he had been.

And he had absolutely no desire to experience that ever again.

The morning of the work trip to Finley Towers Leah woke feeling utterly exhausted. The last few shifts had been chaotic, with A&E overrun with people, ambulances queuing outside, patients waiting in corridors on trolleys. There hadn't even seemed to be time for a break, to grab a cup of tea or use the toilet. In fact she could barely remember eating yesterday at all. There'd been that half a bagel she'd grabbed for breakfast before she'd started her shift, but after that…

No wonder she felt tired! She was running on empty.

But today would be a day for recharging her batteries, having fun and filling up on hot dogs and burgers and candy floss. Whatever she wanted. This was going to be a treat. She loved theme parks and she'd never been to Finley Towers.

There were eight of them going, including Ben and herself, so it ought to be fun, getting to know everyone out of the hospital environment. They could relax and kick back. Laugh. Just enjoy themselves.

It was something she hadn't done for a long time, what

with prepping herself for parenthood, going through all those hormone treatments to try and produce a good egg for the Petri dish... Working... Moving to a new area where she wanted to finally put down some roots and say, *Hey, this is me.*

It had all been so adult and serious. Now she had some time in which she could regress a bit. Have fun.

That was why she had slept with Ben. Why she had decided to cut loose for once in her life and just go for it! She'd wanted some fun—for herself. To forget about all the stresses and strains that were going on in her life, to forget about her desire to start a family and go out there and *live*. To make a connection with someone for the pure joy of it.

Maybe it was a selfish reason, but it had seemed right at the time. And Ben had been...well, perfect. Fun, cheeky, sexy and desirable.

And my boss!

That fact still made her smile. It had been awkward, finding out, but these last couple of weeks had shown her another side to him. He was honest and kind, intelligent—and a hard worker. Just yesterday she'd found him still at the hospital, long after his shift should have ended.

'Hey, what are you still doing here?' she'd asked.

'Oh, I just popped in to check on someone.'

'Who?'

'Mrs Clark, who we admitted yesterday. She's up on E4 after her stroke. Thought I'd check on her.'

'Mrs Clark? The little old lady from the Meadows Care Home?'

He'd nodded. 'She mentioned she was alone. I thought she seemed quite frightened. Thought it might be nice for her to see a friendly face.'

That was nice. It showed he was caring...

Outside, she heard the beep of a horn and grabbed her bag and hurried out. Everyone was waving at her from the small mini-bus someone had hired, and they all cheered as she slid open the door and clambered inside. There was one seat left and it was next to Ben.

'Hi!' she said, getting into the seat and fastening the seatbelt.

'Hi. You look nice.'

'Oh, this old thing?'

It wasn't an old thing at all. She'd gone out to buy it on purpose, wanting a nice new top to wear with her usual jeans.

She suspected he wanted to say something else, but surrounded by their colleagues—and no doubt knowing how quickly the hospital grapevine worked—he chose just to smile instead.

'How long should it take us to get there?'

'An hour. Maybe two. Depending upon traffic.'

'Okay.'

She smiled at him, but he looked awkward and unsure. Just gave her another quick smile and then looked out of the window again. Had she upset him, somehow? He'd been the one to ask if she was free to come along on this trip. Was he regretting it?

She sat awkwardly alongside him, occasionally talking to the others, hoping he might join in. But he didn't. The urge to reach out and lay her hand on his, ask him if he was all right, was difficult to fight.

In the end she managed to lean in and whisper, 'Are you all right?'

He'd nodded, smiled. 'Sure.'

'You're very quiet.'

'Sorry. Just tired. Ignore me.'

But that was an impossible instruction. 'No. I won't.

You're here to have fun, just like the rest of us, and I won't let you *pretend* you're enjoying yourself. I'm going to make you. All right?'

He laughed, nodding his head. 'All right. Thank you.'

The traffic was kind and they managed to get there in just under ninety minutes. They parked, got tickets, and filed through into the park.

Their first port of call was The Precipice—a rollercoaster that slowly climbed up to a peak before dropping over the edge into an inverted twisted dive.

She'd heard about it, and had always wanted to go on it, and they all hurried into the queue.

'A patient told me about this ride. Said it scared the living daylights out of him!' she said.

'So heights don't bother you?' Ben asked.

'No. Do they bother *you*?'

He shook his head. 'No.'

'Good. You can sit with me, then. At the front, if we can—I want the best view of that drop!'

He smiled at her, amused. 'You're twisted, Dr Hudson.'

She laughed at the look on his face. 'Haven't you heard, Mr Willoughby? All the best people are.'

She looked up as a couple of cars slowly chugged up the track, loaded with passengers, then watched as it ascended to its very apex, beaming with joy as everyone screamed as they were pitched over the edge.

What was the view like from up there? She pulled her mobile from her pocket to take a picture, then leaned into Ben. 'Selfie?'

He leaned in towards her and smiled, and she clicked to take the photo.

'I'll email you any good ones.'

'Thanks.'

But she noticed he looked uncertain. Uncomfortable? Was she forcing too much of herself upon him? Perhaps. She knew that sometimes she could be a bit much. Wearing her heart on her sleeve. Keeping the people she cared about close.

Perhaps she ought to remember that even though she'd slept with this man, and wanted more, they could never be together like that. Their lives were on two different paths.

I should give him some space.

But the queue was long and eager, and they were pushed together, shuffling closer, physically within each other's space. And before they knew it, it was their turn.

She and Ben clambered into the front car, grinning madly at their luck as the harness was clamped down over their shoulders, clicking into place. Her stomach was rolling with excitement and she grabbed the handles and looked at the track in front of her.

Who'd have thought a few weeks ago that she'd be doing *this* with her one-night stand? The guy she'd thought she would never see again?

All her previous exhaustion was gone, her lethargy replaced by excitement and anticipation. She hadn't been on a rollercoaster for years, but she remembered the thrill. That surge of excitement at what was about to happen. She'd felt it that night with Ben, too. But that had been different. More potent. This, what she was feeling now, was…

Something's not right.

What was it? What was bothering her? *Something.* Something she felt she ought to know, but didn't.

She glanced at Ben and saw he was looking at her.

'You okay? You suddenly look…different.'

'I'm fine!' she lied, trying to think just what the hell

it was she was supposed to be figuring out. To put her finger on the doubt that was suddenly niggling at her.

The guy in charge of the ride went to his booth and pressed the start button and their car began to rattle forward.

She risked a quick nervous glance at Ben and realised she felt sick. Sick with nerves. She'd never felt this way before. Was it because she was here with him? Because they were doing something as friends when she ought not to be starting anything with him?

Am I starting something? Hoping for it?

Up and up and up went the car, its wheels clacking ominously over the track. The sense of gravity pulling at her made her stomach churn and toss as her heart hammered in her chest and her hands gripped the handles tighter than before, the whiteness of her knuckles showing through.

Why am I scared? I'm never scared. Excited, yes, but scared...?

She pressed her feet into the base of the car, trying to ground herself, trying to get some perspective. Her gaze locked on to the part of the track where it disappeared from sight. They were so close. The drop was coming.

'Ben, I think I'm going to be sick.'

He glanced at her. 'I thought you were okay with heights?'

'I am! I...' She didn't know what it was. *Why* she felt like this. It was unsettling. Terrifying.

'It's too late now. Hold my hand.'

Ben held out his hand for her and she stared at it, then tore her gaze from his hand to the drop. *His hand. The drop. His hand. The drop.* It was close. *Too* close.

She reached for his hand just as the car teetered on the precipice. 'Ben? I—'

She didn't get to finish her sentence. The ride took them over the edge, and her scream mixed with the whoosh of air and the force pinning her into her seat as the car inverted and twisted to the left, zooming down towards the ground in a stomach-dropping nosedive, before it suddenly pulled up and levelled out.

Behind her, everyone was cheering and laughing, but all Leah could focus on was how terrified she was and just how much she was crushing Ben's hand. She squeezed her eyes shut—not wanting to see, not wanting to know. Inside, she felt terrible as she was thrown this way and that, on a never-ending ride of bumps and jerks, and then…it slowed.

She opened her eyes, felt her cheeks wet.

'You're crying.' Ben was looking at her with concern.

'No. I'm not.' She dabbed at her eyes to check, but he was right. She *was* crying! Her cheeks were damp with her tears. 'Oh!'

The car pulled to a halt and the harness was lifted. And then she was out and stumbling from the ride, and before she knew it she was being sick into a rubbish bin. The bin stank of old hot dogs and chips and cigarettes. And now bile.

Someone was holding her hair back.

'You're okay. I've got you.'

Ben! Oh, my God, this is so embarrassing! All that brave talk about loving rollercoasters! They'll all think I was lying...

She retched again.

Rollercoasters never made her sick. Why had this one done so? Was it because she had felt real fear? But *why*?

In the periphery of her vision she saw a tissue being handed to her. She took it and wiped her mouth.

'Thanks.'

She stood up, one hand on her stomach, and let Ben help her towards a bench. The others all gathered around, too.

'Perhaps you shouldn't have had breakfast, Leah?'

'Maybe just the kiddies' rides for you from now on.'

She smiled bravely. 'I'm all right. You all carry on. I'll just sit here for a moment to catch my breath.'

'I'll sit with you.'

'No, it's okay, Ben. You go on. I'll catch up in a minute.'

'I'm not leaving you behind.'

He sat beside her and put his arm around her shoulder. He was warm and solid.

Leah managed a smile of thanks, grateful for his support. This was *weird*. What had just happened? Where had that fear come from?

'I'll get you a drink. What would you like? Tea? Coffee?'

She shuddered. The thought of them made her stomach churn once again. 'Just water, thanks.'

'Okay.'

She watched him walk over to a booth that was doing a fine business in doughnuts and candy floss, the aromas of which were *not* helping her nausea.

He stood there, tall and handsome, waiting his turn in the queue, and she noted that when a gaggle of young women walked by he didn't even turn to look at them, the way she'd suspected he might—a man like him, with a reputation as a Lothario. She would have suspected a quick glance, a second or two to size them up, see which one he fancied.

When he came back with the water he sat down beside her and rubbed her back. 'Feeling any better?'

'A little, yes. Thank you.'

'Good. You worried me there for a moment.'

'I did?' She liked the fact that he'd been worried. That was nice. It showed he cared about her. So something good had come out of this.

'Yes... I've never seen you look so scared.'

'I've never *felt* so scared. I'm not even sure where it came from.'

Her life had been up in the air these last few weeks, though, hadn't it? Moving home. Getting a new job. Sally's pregnancy. Knowing she was about to become a mother. Meeting Ben. The sexual tension each time she was with him.

Had it all just caught up with her? Or was there something else she wasn't seeing? *What?*

Leah tried to think. Had she felt more stressed lately? She'd thought she was coping admirably, despite all the new pressures and strains. As a doctor, she knew that stress—both good and bad—could have a physical effect on the human body. It could play with hormones, blood pressure, monthly cycles...

She sipped some more water as silently she did some mental maths. Period maths.

Her period was due on the...

She froze.

I'm late. Oh, my God. I'm nearly a week late! Could I be...? No. It's not possible. Is it? No, I can't be! I'm being ridiculous!

CHAPTER FIVE

HE WASN'T SURE how things had changed. He'd been thrown by how concerned he'd felt for her when she'd got ill, and he wasn't sure how to feel about that. Clearly it had been the rollercoaster ride. Lots of people got queasy on rides. It happened all the time.

'How are you feeling now?'

She was sitting on the bench, leaning forward, her elbows on her knees, both hands clutching the water bottle that she was sipping from.

'A bit better, I guess.'

'Did you eat breakfast?'

She nodded.

'And this has never happened to you before?'

It had been a stunning ride. The Precipice had promised them stomach-turning plummets and thrilling twists and turns. Perhaps it had just been too much for her? It was one of the newer rides at the park, and it seemed theme parks these days were bending over backwards to find the scariest rides to bring in more customers.

'No.'

She looked pale, still. He reached for her wrist to take her pulse.

'What are you doing?' She pulled her hand away.

'Checking you over.'

'I'm fine!' She got up and walked away from him, on still quite wobbly legs. 'I'm not sick.'

He sighed. Clearly she was going to be a difficult patient. But what doctor wasn't?

'Shall we catch up with the others?'

She nodded, and together they walked through the crowds, trying to catch up with their colleagues, who had drifted away whilst he tended to Leah. They found everyone gathered around a machine, whilst Richard, one of the nurses, attempted to use a dangling hook to try and grab a teddy bear.

He missed.

'Who's up for the teacups? A little gentler on the senses for Vomit Girl over here!' someone suggested, smiling at her to show it was a joke.

'I might get sick again. No, thanks.' She folded her arms and wouldn't let anyone jolly her along into the queue.

'Are you sure?' asked Ben.

'Maybe later. When my stomach's calmer.'

He saw her watch them. Rollercoaster after rollercoaster she stood there, watching them, her eyes on them but her thoughts clearly a million miles away. Being ill like that had really upset her.

'You sure you're okay?' he asked.

'I'm fine! Honestly. I just don't want to risk getting sick again.'

He accepted that. No one liked being ill.

By the time it got to lunchtime and they all sat down in one of the cafeterias to eat she almost seemed her normal self. But Ben could sense her withdrawal. She was there physically, but not mentally, pushing salad leaves around on her plate to make it look as if she'd eaten.

The rest of the day wasn't what he wanted it to be for

her. Leah became the person to hold coats and bags and phones, standing there like a pack mule whilst everyone else had fun. He hated it that she was being left out, so he stopped going on the rides too, so that he could stand with her.

'You don't have to, you know,' she said.

'I know. But I want to.'

As they were driving home, sitting at the back of the bus together, everyone else fell asleep.

He took her hand in his hesitantly, then squeezed it. 'I'm sorry you got sick.'

'That's okay.' She stared back at him and in the darkness, with just the light from the streetlamps illuminating them, her eyes looked wide and afraid. Why? Because he was holding her hand? Or something else?

But what?

She turned away and pulled her hand free, calling to the driver. 'Richard, would you mind dropping me off in the High Street? I just need to pick up a few things before going home.'

'Sure. Want us to wait for you?'

'No, no. That won't be necessary.'

'We'll wait for you.' Ben said. 'We don't want you walking home alone in the dark.'

'It's literally around the corner. Just a few steps. There's no need for anyone to wait.'

Today was meant to have been a day of fun, and although it had been great for everyone else, he wished he could have got her to include herself more. But she'd held back. Restricting her fun on her only day off. He felt a little guilty for having suggested she come along and be with everyone. Perhaps she felt embarrassed at getting sick in front of everyone after saying she was fine with rollercoasters? What had made her so sick today?

He looked out of the minibus window, watching as she hurried away to the shops.

Leah closed the front door behind her and sank back against it, her eyes closed, as she took a minute just to breathe.

The closer they had got to home, and the closer she had got to the shops, she had found her breath hitching in her throat, becoming shallow as she fought to steady her nerves and her anxiety.

She *couldn't* be pregnant! It was something that she could never risk happening. Her doctors had told her so many times that it would be near impossible, if not futile, to believe that she would carry a child normally.

And with Ben right beside her—the man whose sperm might have achieved a miracle—she had felt nervier still.

As she'd stood there all day, watching her colleagues go on ride after ride, her gaze had kept travelling to the warning signs by each ride.

Anyone with a heart issue...

If you're pregnant...

She couldn't tell him what was worrying her. She couldn't share her concern. Because it was stupid, right? The idea that she might be pregnant? It was probably just motion sickness she'd had, or perhaps there'd been something a little off with that cold pasta she'd shovelled down for breakfast that morning? It could be all manner of things.

But nothing had felt stranger—ever—than standing in that supermarket, staring at the pregnancy test kits on the shelves.

She'd never paid them much heed before. Had grieved

briefly that she would never get to use one, but that had been all. So to pick one up and put it in her basket had felt...*secretive*. Forbidden. Reckless! Was she allowing herself to even think that it was a possibility? She was convinced that she was about to have her vain hopes crushed. Why punish herself?

She'd not even been able to meet the gaze of the girl on the till, knowing that if she saw any question or excitement in the girl's eyes it would be all too much.

She could barely dare to hope herself, never mind deal with anyone else's questions.

He doesn't like kids. He never wants to be a father.

He'd told her those things. No matter what happened when she peed on that testing stick, she could not expect anything from him.

Oh, my God, I could have two babies! The baby Sally is carrying and another...

She lifted her bag and rummaged through it, pulling out the testing kit and staring at it. There were two testing sticks inside.

She finally managed to find the energy to take her shopping into the kitchen and put everything away. Then she filled the kettle to make something hot to drink. Not tea. The idea of tea was... She shuddered. Nauseating.

Hot chocolate. That was what she wanted.

She spooned cocoa into a mug and turned to look at the pregnancy test kit sitting on the kitchen surface.

Should I take it now? Or first thing in the morning?

There would be a more accurate reading from morning urine. If there was any hCG to detect at all. If she took one tonight she wouldn't trust it, and then she'd waste the second one, so...

Leah made her hot chocolate and placed the kit in her

bathroom. She would use it tomorrow. First thing. Right before work. And then she would know.

She sat back in bed, clutching her mug of cocoa, and wondered if she would get any sleep at all.

I could call Sally.

She would know what to do. What to say.

But I don't even know if I am pregnant! It's probably best to wait and see what the test says. I can call her tomorrow.

The hours stretched out ahead of her...

She woke with a start as her alarm burst into song on the bedside cabinet beside her. Slapping her palm down on it, she cut off the noise of the radio and slowly sat upright, rubbing at eyes that felt sore and tired.

She'd stayed awake for a long time, staring at the ceiling, telling herself over and over that it was best to wait. That if she did the test then she would only experience crushing disappointment if it was negative and never get to sleep, or get no sleep at all if it was positive, because that would be terrifying, and she would have to keep it to herself for hours, and then she would be fit to bursting, so...

Now, with a sense of dread, like a prisoner approaching the gallows, she made a slow shuffle into the bathroom and switched on the light. She felt a sense of disbelief. The one thing that she couldn't allow to happen might have actually happened. The one thing she had always dreamed of doing—carrying her own child—might possibly be happening.

But that would be terrible! Because she'd been told she couldn't carry a child. Not to term. She would lose it in the second trimester. It might not even develop properly! There was an incredibly slim chance that everything would go well, but that chance was minute, and she'd not had much luck in her life so far—why would that be any different?

There were deep shadows beneath her eyes when she looked in the mirror and she looked exhausted. But there it still sat. The testing kit. Exactly where she'd left it.

It hadn't been a dream.

She hadn't imagined the events of yesterday.

Picking it up, she read the instructions and carried them out, placing the testing stick on the toilet cistern as she washed her hands, her heart thundering in her chest as snakes coiled in her stomach.

What am I even doing? This is ridiculous! I can't be pregnant. I'm just letting fear run away with me yet again!

She'd had a lot of fear growing up. Had let it make her wish for things. To be fostered. To find her real parents. To find a home where she could put down roots. And then she had worried that all those things would go terribly wrong.

She'd hoped that the doctors were wrong.

But she was grown up now. Had already taken her future destiny into her own hands. She had a surrogate! She would be a mother in a few short months! There was a baby already on the way—a little girl.

She would be perfect. All she needed.

I don't need this test to be positive. I'm already getting what I've always wanted. I'm already going to be a mother. It can be negative. I don't care.

She picked up the test and looked at it.

She blinked and stared a little harder, her heart racing as her legs began to feel weak and shaky.

There were two lines. Two solid blue lines.

I'm pregnant.

* * *

The peeing. It had to be psychosomatic, right? Ever since those blue lines had appeared Leah had felt the need to pee every hour or so—which was ridiculous, considering that normally she could work a twelve-hour shift and not need the loo once.

My bladder must be the size of an ant's!

And her boobs hurt. And her feet ached. Could you get swollen ankles in the first trimester?

Probably. If you tried hard enough.

But more than anything she found herself craving hummus. Of all things, her body wanted the humble chickpea in an effort to control her nausea.

She was finding concentrating difficult—which wasn't surprising, considering she'd just discovered something terrifying about herself and could tell no one. Well, there was *one* person she ought to tell, but he would no doubt run a mile the second she began to say the words. She wouldn't even get to the second syllable without him wanting to run screaming for the hills.

Ben was a good guy—he just wasn't father material. He'd told her that. This was something she was going to have to do alone.

And with her other baby, of course.

Two babies under the age of one if mine survives. They'll be like twins.

The urge to see her GP strengthened. She needed to talk to *someone* about this. Leah got out her mobile to call Sally. Her friend would know what to do. What to say. But when she called no one answered the phone, and that was when she remembered that Sally, her husband and three children had gone away for a few days. A camping trip they'd booked ages ago.

Damn!

Instead she called her GP surgery and asked for an emergency appointment. There was an appointment with the duty doctor if she went straight away, so she made another quick call to work, to say she might be a few minutes late.

She sat in the waiting room, twiddling her thumbs, checking her mobile, staring at all the worn and torn posters on the wall of the surgery telling people to stop smoking, or advising women to get mammograms.

She couldn't quite believe she was in this situation—not knowing what was happening or what she could do about it. She had never expected ever to get pregnant in her entire life. It was the whole reason she'd got a surrogate. But now that she was…the idea of having to terminate terrified her.

Because what if there was a chance?

The screen in front of her flashed up her name.

Leah Hudson. Dr Dempsey. Room 4.

She hurried in, smiling at the young woman in front of her.

'How can I help?'

Where to start? 'I did a pregnancy test this morning and it was positive.'

'Oh. Okay. And how do you feel about that?'

'Terrified. Shocked. Numb.'

'Would you like me to explain your options?'

'No. I know my options. I'm a doctor. Emergency medicine. It's just that… I have a bicornuate uterus and I was told that I probably wouldn't be able to carry a baby past the second trimester, or that there would be developmental concerns, so I don't know what to do. I never thought I'd get pregnant. I never wanted to take that risk!'

Dr Dempsey nodded sagely. 'Have you had a scan of your uterus?'

'A long time ago.'

'Let me take a look.' She turned to the computer and pressed a few keys, scrolling through the information she had in front of her, bringing up the images of the scan that Leah had had done years ago.

'Okay, so that's quite a split you have there. You see how the uterus has two horn-like projections?'

Leah nodded.

'I think you probably need to be seen by a specialist who can advise you better. When was your last period?'

Leah gave her the date.

'So you're about six weeks? Okay. It's too soon to scan your uterus right now and see whereabouts the embryo has implanted. If you want the baby, you need to hope that it's implanted down here, where there's room for it to develop normally, but I have to warn you that there's a strong chance that—'

'That it's implanted in one of the horns?'

The doctor nodded. 'I'll make a referral for you and see if we can get an early scan, and then you can make an informed decision.'

'About whether to terminate or not?'

Dr Dempsey nodded. 'I'm sorry.'

'It's not your fault.'

Leah gave a brave smile, but inside she felt no bravery at all. There was an extremely small chance that her baby would be all right. So small she didn't even want to try and calculate the percentage.

'So what do I do in the meantime?'

Dr Dempsey shook her head. 'You wait, and hope for the best.'

* * *

The fear hovered in her brain as she sat suturing the leg of a young girl who had caught it on barbed wire and thought the best way to free herself would be to yank it out, which had caused much tearing of the skin. The wound was jagged—like a river of red.

Leah knotted the final stitch and checked her work, satisfied, as she removed her gloves. 'Right, I'll call for a nurse to come and put a dressing on that and then you'll be free to go.'

'Can I walk on it?'

'Yes, but you'll need to rest it too. I don't recommend a marathon shopping expedition.'

'What about getting it wet?'

'We'll give you some waterproof dressings, so that you can still shower, but try and keep it dry for the next week or so. You'll need to see your GP in about ten to fourteen days to have the stitches removed.'

'Thanks.'

'No problem.' She disposed of all her used materials in the clinical waste bin and washed her hands, then picked up her patient file and left the cubicle to fill out her notes.

Her bladder reminded her of its presence and she made a quick detour to the staff loo after putting her file on the desk to return to afterwards.

She hadn't seen Ben yet. Someone had said he was in a meeting when she'd got there first thing, and she'd been glad of the reprieve. Whether he was involved or not, she was about to change his life—and she wasn't looking forward to seeing the need to escape in his eyes.

She wasn't ready for that, yet.

Maybe I should wait to tell him. Until I know what's happening. What I should do.

Leah stared at her reflection in the mirror and considered the possibilities. Was it cowardly to wait? Or common sense? Should she just tell him right now, so that there was someone else with whom she could share the burden?

The burden? *He's got me thinking in his terms! And I'm not sure I want to see the rejection in his eyes.*

This baby wasn't a burden. It was a miracle. And Ben was the father of that miracle and he deserved to know it existed. They'd created a baby together and that was something special. He needed to know about it, right? Even if the baby might not make it?

She patted her face with water and then dried it with a paper towel.

I'll tell him when I see him next. When he's got a spare moment and we can be alone.

Leah left the bathroom and headed back to the doctors' desk. She grabbed her patient's file and began writing. Her hands were trembling slightly. She hadn't noticed during suturing, but she noticed it now. It had to be anxiety.

She glanced up to take a deep breath—and saw Ben striding along a corridor, away from her.

Her heart leapt into her throat at that brief glimpse of him—the father of her child—his broad stride, his strong legs. She remembered the shape of them. The feel of them against her own bare skin.

That night had been so special, but neither of them had truly known how much. And *he* had no idea just how much she was about to change his life.

Her hand went to her belly.

'You still feel sick?' It was Richard, who had driven the minibus. 'You look pale.'

She instantly beamed a smile and shook her head. 'Nope! I'm all good. Feeling good. Definitely A-Okay. You?'

He laughed at her overreaction. 'I'm fine. Have you… er…got a thing with Mr Willoughby? I notice you spend a lot of time talking to each other. Seems like you get along.'

'Oh, no, nothing like that.'

'You sure? Only I'd hate for him to break your heart. There's one or two ladies around who will tell you not to touch him with an extra-long bargepole.'

She nodded as if she understood totally. 'Oh, I've heard. Don't you worry about me—he's just a friend.'

Now, why couldn't that have sounded more convincing?

'He's a great guy—don't get me wrong—but…' Richard smiled. 'He…er…tends to be just a first-date kind of guy. A *look-for-someone-new* kind of guy. He's not the commitment type. And I only say that because you're a friend, and you're nice, and…' Now he looked a bit more uncomfortable. 'You don't…er…fancy going for a drink one night? Just you and me?'

Leah blushed as she realised what he was propositioning. 'Well, that's very nice of you, Richard, but…um… I'm not really looking to date anyone right now. Things are complicated, so…' She let her voice trail off, hoping he wasn't too offended at being let down.

'No worries. No harm in asking, right?'

'No, not at all!'

'Better get on. I'll see you around.' And he disappeared.

'Yes, see you around.' She watched him go and let out a breath.

Wow. If only he knew…

CHAPTER SIX

HE'D BEEN LOOKING for her everywhere. Minors. Majors. Resus. She was definitely in today, but where?

'Tina, have you seen Dr Hudson?'

The healthcare assistant thought for a moment, her brow furrowing. 'I think she's gone on her break.'

'Right. Thanks.'

That meant she could be anywhere. The hospital shop…maybe the cafeteria or the staff room. He decided to check the latter first, but she was nowhere to be seen and he huffed out a sigh in frustration.

He *had* to know how she was today. He'd got almost no sleep last night, thinking about her, tossing and turning and getting caught up in his bedsheets until he'd thrown them off in anger. He'd told himself he had no reason to worry about her. She was fine. She'd just got sick, that was all, and she wasn't his to worry over.

Ben strode down the corridor towards the hospital shop and peered inside—she wasn't there. He was just about to head to the cafeteria when he happened to glance out of one of the windows. He saw a figure on one of the benches outside, nursing a drink.

Leah.

His pulse thrummed as he did an about-turn and

headed outside. He had to go and see her. He *had* to. He didn't understand why, but the compulsion was strong.

Outside, there was a small remembrance garden. Just a circle, really, with a willow tree in the centre, some flowerbeds and a circle of benches looking in.

Leah sat alone, sipping from a cup, and now he could see she also had a small dipping pot of hummus and some carrot sticks, too.

'Hi.'

She turned quickly, startled, and her drink sloshed over the rim of her cup and spattered all over her scrubs.

'Sorry. You okay? I didn't mean to startle you.'

She was blushing and wiping her legs. 'Well, at least it wasn't a hot drink. I guess that's something.' She gave him an awkward smile and then looked away.

'May I sit with you?'

She nodded. 'Of course.' She moved her hummus pot and carrot sticks to the arm of the bench so that he could sit beside her.

'You've found a nice quiet spot.'

Leah smiled. 'We all need a little stillness sometimes.'

'I agree.'

Neither of them said anything for a moment, but he spent that time staring at her, trying to read her. She was eating, so that was good. Clearly her appetite was back and she wasn't feeling sick any more.

He leant back against the bench and stretched out his legs, feeling some of his cares lift away. It was soothing to be with her, somehow.

'It was a strange old day yesterday, wasn't it?' she asked.

He laughed. 'It sure was.'

'Me getting sick…'

'Do you feel better now?'

'Yes.' She blushed and looked away, her glance falling on the hummus before she looked back at him again. 'And no.'

He frowned.

'Yesterday was…scary.'

He nodded. 'That ride was rough.'

'I wasn't talking about the ride.'

What did she mean?

'I realised something yesterday. Something important. Something…terrifying.'

Whatever it was, he could tell she was gathering up all her courage to tell him about it. He laid his hand on hers, honoured that she felt she could tell him. 'What is it?' he asked gently.

'I'm late.' She bit her lip and stared at him, willing him to make the connection.

'Late?' Ben sat up straighter, staring hard at her. What was she saying? He needed her to be clear. 'What do you mean?'

He could feel his heart begin to thud as his thoughts ran in one direction. Faster and faster. He could feel his stomach twist and turn in apprehension. *It couldn't be.*

'I did a test. This morning.'

'A test?' He had to be sure they were talking about the same thing.

'A…a *pregnancy* test.'

Pow, pow, pow! He could hear his pulse in his ears. His legs were feeling weird, somehow boneless.

He swallowed hard, knowing the answer but needing to hear it anyway, because there might just be a minute chance that he was wrong…

'And?'

'And it was positive.'

She laughed suddenly. Hysterically. A sound of un-adulterated surprise, shock and disbelief.

'I'm pregnant, Ben!'

But then her smile disappeared and she looked ter-rified again.

He stared hard at her, trying to make sense of it all and struggling. Pregnant? But she'd said she couldn't carry a baby. Not to term, anyway. And she was already going to have a baby with the help of this friend of hers.

'And I'm the father?'

'Yes! I don't make it a habit to sleep around, *Mr* Wil-loughby.' She sounded hurt.

'No, of course not. I'm sorry.'

'You're shocked. I get that. I knew you would be. So am I. It's not exactly what you hoped and dreamed of, is it?'

'I...' He really had no idea what to say.

Yes, it was a shock. And he had no idea what they were going to do about it.

He got up and began pacing, his hands on his hips.

Leah watched him, biting her lip, nervous of how he might react. She knew this wasn't what he wanted, and now he was being faced with the reality of it.

'You're—what?—about six weeks along?'

'Something like that, yes.'

He stopped pacing and turned directly to look at her. 'How do you feel?'

'Terrified. I saw a doctor this morning. She said I have to wait for my first scan, so we can try and judge where-abouts the baby has implanted and whether it'll...' Her voice tailed off as she stared ahead of her, not willing to finish the thought.

He looked at her, understanding. 'Whether it'll survive?'

She nodded and wiped a tear from her eye. 'I never

thought this was possible and yet it is. It's happened.' She smiled at him. 'You are the father and I thought it only right that you know. Even if it doesn't make it.'

He flinched, remembering all she had said about her inability to carry a child to term. What was going on here? How had this happened? They'd been so careful.

Ben sank onto the bench next to her. 'When will you know?'

'When they can fit me in for a scan. The GP said it would be too early to tell right now anyway. We might not be able to pick up a heartbeat yet. It needs to grow a bit, I think, for us to know for sure.'

'And when we do?'

'Then we make the decision. Of what's best for the child.'

He nodded. Of course. He let his thoughts wander. There was a moment of quiet between them that was filled by birdsong and the low hum of traffic beyond them as people searched for car parking spaces.

Leah was pregnant. With his baby. It might not survive. And not only was she pregnant, there was another baby going to be born. Carried by this Sally.

'Two babies…' He shook his head, glanced at the willow tree, grabbed some of its hanging fronds and swished them away from him, watching as they fell neatly back into place. If only life was as simple.

'Yes. The next few months are going to be tough—for both of us—but, hey, I'm a doctor in A&E. I'm used to being tough.' She tried to laugh. Tried to make light of it. 'So I'll be okay.'

Was she trying to convince herself of that?

Ben didn't smile. He clearly didn't find it funny.

'I can't believe this. We were careful. We used protection.'

She nodded, waiting patiently, as if for a verdict to

come in. Would he find himself *Not Guilty* and say he wanted nothing to do with this and walk away? Or would he accept his part in all this and agree to be there for her? For *them*?

'I know you had a difficult childhood, Ben, and that this is hard for you—'

'That's just it!' he blurted in frustration. 'I didn't actually *get* a childhood! I was the father my siblings should have had. I was the mother. I was the one who waited for them after school to walk them home. I was the one who had to cook the dinner and wash up and help them with their homework. I was the one who got them to bed and sat with them when they had nightmares, and I was the one who got them up again and ready for school. *I shouldn't have had to do that.* I shouldn't have had to clear up the mess my parents left behind.'

'You had it rough. I know that—'

'Do you know they went away on their own? For a whole weekend my parents just upped and left us. No warning. No money left behind for food. We had to make do with what little was in the cupboards and the freezer. I should have hated it—but you know what? It was one of the best weekends we ever had. Because Mum and Dad weren't there, spoiling it with their weed and their beer, snoring loudly on the couch and stinking the place out. We were fine by ourselves! We didn't need them. The best day of my entire life was when I moved out to go to university. I paid my own way—working in bars and restaurants, two jobs, double shifts—but it was all worth it, because all I had to think about was *me*.'

'And those left behind?'

That guilt was still there. Still painful. Walking away—leaving—and knowing that he was leaving them to fend for themselves without him, their older brother, there to shelter them from the worst of it.

'A neighbour eventually reported my parents to Social Services. They made sure those kids were looked after and they got fostered. It killed me that I never did that for them, and I live with that every day.' He sighed. 'Parents are fallible. They're human and they make mistakes. But being a parent is such an important job—'

'One that *you* got right.'

'Maybe. But it wasn't my role. It never should have been. And I've always told myself I would never have it again. The worries. The concern. The sleepless nights…'

'You're telling me you can't do this?'

'I'm not saying that, no. I'm just…venting.'

She smiled. 'I understand. And I'm sorry you had such a terrible start, but so did I. I've always wanted to have a family of my own because I've always been cast out. I was left in a bin as a baby. That's how little my parents thought of me. But I want to be the best mother in the world. To give my children what I never had— love, security, a warm home where they can feel safe and cherished.'

He looked at her. 'It sounds like you've already made up your mind.'

'I'd like to think that if the pregnancy is viable then I can do this. It's all I've ever wanted—to be a mother.'

She could see he was considering what she'd said.

'But if you can't do it, then I'm giving you an out. No pressure. No blame.'

Leah got up from her seat, gathering her things together, ready to head back inside. She'd been out here long enough and she was beginning to feel the cold.

'I understand that this isn't a perfect situation and it's a shock to us both.'

She'd just got to the double doors that would let her in to the department when he chased after her and called out. 'Wait!'

She turned around and looked up at him with blurry eyes.

He smiled at her, wiped away the tears that ran down her cheeks and said, 'I need time.'

She smiled. 'You have it. Honestly, Ben. There's no pressure here. Though it would be nice if you were involved. I like you. I do. A lot.'

He liked her, too. Probably more than he should. And now they were involved more than he'd ever thought he would be with a woman. But if it was going to be with anyone, then he was glad it was with her. They had some difficult times ahead, but they could support one another and get through it, no matter what happened.

He hugged her, pressing her against his chest, feeling her heartbeat thundering away within her ribcage and loving the way her being in his arms made him feel. Safe. Warm. Secure.

No longer alone.

A part of something.

Protective once again.

He'd thought it would feel wrong.

But for some strange reason it felt, oh, so *right*.

CHAPTER SEVEN

'PEDESTRIAN VERSUS CAR, travelling at approximately forty miles an hour. Obvious bull's-eye on the windscreen and an anterior head laceration. Query broken ribs and right femur. No known allergies, but confirmed COPD and Type Two diabetes. Two of morphine. BP is low at ninety over sixty, pulse ninety-six and SATs at eighty-eight.'

Max, the paramedic, helped transfer their new patient onto the bed with a backboard slide, and then he and his partner wheeled away their equipment after handing over their treatment form to Ben.

Leah began checking the man's airway as the rest of the Majors team busied themselves around the patient like ants around a discarded sweet.

Venous access was gained, blood gases taken, pelvis stability checked. Airway. Breathing. Circulation.

Their patient, a man in his late eighties, was conscious.

'Is there anyone we can call for you, Joe?'

Joe coughed and winced. 'My wife, Nancy.' He told them her telephone number.

Leah looked up at Ben. 'We're going to need a chest X-ray.'

'We'll get it done here. Call Radiology.'

She nodded and headed to the red phone on the wall, on which she asked for someone to operate the portable

X-ray machine they had in the department. Then she adjusted Joe's nasal cannula and checked the oxygen levels going in.

He couldn't have it on a high flow because of his COPD—Chronic Obstructive Pulmonary Disease. It needed to be low, because too high a flow would cause oxygen toxicity, and the increased retention of carbon dioxide could slow his breathing and cause drowsiness. It might even cause respiratory acidosis and be fatal if not managed properly. It was a fine balancing act with a COPD patient.

'How are you feeling?' she asked him.

'A bit banged up. But I crashed a plane once and I survived that, so I guess I'll survive this little knock.'

She smiled. 'You crashed a plane?'

'A private plane. It wasn't a passenger jet or anything.'

'Wow.'

'I had engine failure at twelve thousand feet. Managed to bring the bird down as much as I could, but it was a rough landing.'

'Sounds like it. How long ago was that?'

'About twenty years ago. My wife refused to let me get inside a vehicle ever again. Said they were too dangerous.' He smiled. 'Guess she was right, huh?'

'Lots of things in life are dangerous. We can't avoid them all.'

The radiologist arrived and Leah began to put on one of the lead aprons.

Ben touched her arm. 'What are you doing?'

'Getting gowned up for X-ray.'

He frowned and motioned for her to move away from the other members of staff. 'You're pregnant. I don't want you taking any unnecessary risks.'

She coloured, not wanting anyone else who might

be able to hear to know just yet. 'That's what the apron is for.'

'Maybe so, but I don't want you in here. Step outside for this.'

'He's *my* patient.' She bristled.

'He's *ours*. And he'll cope without you for the five seconds it takes to do the X-ray.'

She felt her cheeks colour. 'Everyone will notice. They'll start asking questions.'

'They're too busy to notice. Please humour me, Leah, and step outside.'

Sighing, she handed him the apron and stepped outside after telling Joe that she would be back in a moment.

She watched them proceed through the small pane of glass in the door, one hand absently holding her abdomen. It was perfectly flat. No obvious signs outwardly. She did have a kind of metallic taste in her mouth that didn't seem to go away, though, and it had stopped her from drinking tea and coffee. And she felt tired early in the evenings, yawning heavily before eight p.m.

And even though she was slightly annoyed—the lead aprons were good protection—she felt torn in two directions. Ben was quite clearly worrying about her well-being. About their baby. He knew that it already had enough battles to face and he was simply trying to protect her, and it, from another.

That was a good sign from a man who had just found he was going to be a dad. Especially one who'd thought he didn't want to be.

Perhaps their situation would be an eye-opener for both of them? From what he'd told her about his past, he'd looked after his younger brother and sister like a father, taking care of all their needs—feeding them, making sure they had clean clothes, making sure they slept. Caring for them when they were ill.

He knew how to do it. He knew how to care.

He wouldn't be a doctor, otherwise!

He could be a great father if he gave himself the chance to be. Perhaps if I tell him that. Encourage him... especially if everything goes okay.

With the X-ray done, she headed back inside the department and rechecked Joe's oxygen SATs. They were at ninety now, so she removed the nasal cannula and turned off the oxygen.

'We'll just take a look at those films and let you know what you've done to yourself, okay?'

Joe nodded. 'Looks like I'm gonna be here for a while.'

Leah smiled at him and patted his hand. 'We'll look after you. It's what we do best.'

And it was. It was the whole purpose of their work. To look after people. Both her and Ben. For a man who never wanted that sort of responsibility, he'd certainly picked an odd job!

We'll get through this. I just know we will.

Joe had fractured a couple of ribs and broken his femur, so he was transferred up to Orthopaedics for an operation in the morning.

Leah, in the meantime, went home and got some rest. These early weeks of pregnancy were meant to be the toughest, and now she could understand why. If she wasn't feeling sick she was feeling exhausted, or she needed to pee, or she craved something weird and wonderful that never seemed to be available in the hospital cafeteria.

At home she could indulge her cravings, and she was just

tucking into a baked sweet potato, drenched in coconut yoghurt and a sprinkling of cinnamon, when the doorbell rang.

She sighed, considering ignoring it and letting whoever it was go away, or at least come back later, but whoever it was kept ringing the bell. And then she heard her letterbox open and a voice call out.

'Leah?'

Ben.

She scooped in a mouthful of food, and then another, before putting the bowl down and answering the front door.

He looked at her and smiled. 'Hi.'

'Hi.'

'Can I come in?'

'Sure!' She stepped back and closed the door behind him and led him into her front room. A room they hadn't really stayed in the last time he was here. She flushed at the thought of it.

'Can I get you something to eat?'

He looked down at her bowl on the table. 'Would it be that? Whatever it is?'

'Sweet potato, coconut yoghurt and cinnamon,' she answered, embarrassed. 'Er...do you want some?'

'Hmm... I'd hoped it was ice cream on the end of your nose.'

Flushing, she wiped her nose and, yes, there was a dab of coconut yoghurt on the side of her finger. She licked it off, grinning. 'Don't judge me. I need it. The baby needs it. It's been telling me so all day.'

He laughed and sat down after she did.

'Cravings already, huh?'

'Tell me about it. I must be lacking in some nutrient. But if the baby wants this, then this is what I shall give it.

I shall give my child anything it wants to make it happy.' Her eyes darkened briefly. 'Whilst I can.'

'We don't want to spoil it.'

She smiled at him as she spooned in another mouthful of food. It really was hitting the spot. 'Nutrients is not spoiling a child.'

'I guess not.' He watched her eat for a moment longer. 'You don't mind that I've popped round? Only we don't really get to talk at work.'

'No. Not a problem. Things get a little frantic at the hospital sometimes. It's nice to talk in an unhurried environment, occasionally.'

'Agreed.'

But as she spooned in more of her mixture she noticed that he wasn't saying anything at all. Nor did he look comfortable. If she had to use a word to describe him she'd use *awkward*. Or *apprehensive*.

It made her lose her appetite, and she put the bowl down and used a napkin to wipe her mouth. 'You okay?'

'I've been thinking about my parents.'

She nodded. Yes, she thought he might have been. This baby had changed everything between them. It would change their futures. Including the fact that he'd believed his would be child-free.

'And what thoughts did you have?'

'That they were out of their depth. That they behaved like children themselves, having all the things in life they shouldn't and no one to tell them no. Maybe that was why they didn't know how to deal with me and the others. They were just kids who liked too much sex, too much booze and too much weed.'

'We meet a lot of those people in A&E.'

He nodded. 'I love my brother and sister, and I love the children they have now—but only at a distance. I took on *so much* responsibility. I used to have sleepless nights. Worrying about what there might be in the cupboards to feed them for breakfast. Whether there'd be enough to make them a packed lunch. I shouldn't have had those worries. I shouldn't have had to take care of everybody. And I began to resent it. I began acting out. Just like my parents. Getting into trouble at school. Picking fights. Stealing from shops.' He shook his head. 'I resented them.'

'And you're worried you'll resent me?'

He ran his hands through his hair. 'I don't want to.'

She smiled politely. 'Well, at least you're being honest. I didn't expect you to jump up and down with glee. But, you know, if it makes you feel any better... I'm scared, too.'

He looked up, tiredness in his eyes. 'I know.'

'I've not had one good parent either—*not one*. I don't know what it is to be a mother.' She bit her lip. 'But I do know I want to do all I can to protect this little one inside me as much as I can, until I have to make a decision. It's a learning process. No one ever said parenthood was easy.'

'Aren't you scared?'

'Ben, I'm *terrified*. This is all I've ever wanted, and now I'm pregnant and faced with the fact that I may have to terminate depending upon where the baby has implanted in my uterus. I'm in the worst lottery ever!'

'I admire you. Your strength and resolve.'

She looked back at him. 'And I admire yours. You don't give yourself much credit for what you did in the past, do you?'

'It had to be done. Someone had to step up.'

She waited for him to realise what he'd said.

He nodded, understanding.

'Do you think you can do it again? Step up?' she asked tentatively.

'If you'd asked me this months ago I would have said no. No way. But since meeting you…and it's you that's carrying my child… I would like to think that I could try.'

She could have cried. Her emotions always seemed at the forefront recently. She felt honoured by his words and his depth of feeling. Clearly he had thought long and hard over this, knowing his past and his fears.

Leah smiled. 'I'm very pleased to hear that.'

'We'll face whatever we have to face.'

She nodded. 'Thank you.'

He was silent for a moment. Then he asked. 'How's everything going with the other pregnancy?'

'Sally? Good. She's been away on a camping trip— which is hilarious, as Sally only usually does five-star accommodation. But she'd promised her boys, so…'

'You make sacrifices for family?'

'Exactly.'

'Have you told her yet? About your pregnancy?'

'No. And I'm desperate to. She's the one I always call. The only person I've ever really relied upon.'

'And the…er…father of that baby?'

'Anonymous sperm donation.'

'Oh. Right.'

'I want a family so much, but I've always been alone, Ben. I've done everything by myself. And so when I decided the time was right to have a child I decided to parent alone, too. Knowing that as long as I just had myself to rely on it wouldn't get screwed up. Silly, I know, but it's how I felt.'

'It's not silly at all.'

'And now I've screwed up. I've got pregnant, knowing

the risks. And I'm scared witless I could lose it!' She began to cry.

Ben shuffled closer and draped his arms around her, holding her trembling body as she cried. He made soft, soothing noises as he stroked her back and her hair, waiting for her to calm and breathe normally again, and when she was finally reduced to just sniffing and holding him tight, he lifted her chin so that she would look at him.

'This wasn't your fault. It was an accident. And though you thought you'd have to do all this alone, know this… I'm *with* you. You don't have to do *any* of this alone any more. I'll keep you safe.'

She smiled and laid her head back against his chest, absorbing the strength of him. The feeling of being secure and looked after. Cared for.

It felt good.

'We're in this together.'

Ben's patient, Amy, had presented with intense abdominal pain and a panicked look in her eyes.

'I'm pregnant! And I can't lose this baby. I can't!'

Beside Amy sat her mother, clutching her hand, and Ben did his best to reassure them as he proceeded with his examination. Amy had no temperature, but her pulse was high, as was her blood pressure—though that could be from anxiety and pain.

'When did the pain start?' he asked as he palpated her abdomen.

'I woke with it. But it wasn't as strong this morning. I took a couple of paracetamol and just got on with things, but by midday it was really beginning to hurt.'

'Did the paracetamol help at all?'

'Not really. It hardly touched it. Please tell me my baby

is going to be okay!' She gripped his wrist to make him look at her and he could see raw fear in her wide eyes.

He had a suspicion as to what it might be. Either an ovarian torsion, a miscarriage, or an ectopic pregnancy. His hunch was on the latter, going by her symptoms.

'I'll need to do an ultrasound. Just give me a moment and I'll get the machine.'

He left the cubicle, relieved to be away from such palpable fear, knowing that maybe he couldn't do a thing about it. And then he saw Leah at the desk, standing by the doctors' station. She looked a little green.

He touched her arm. 'Hey, you okay?'

'Feeling a bit sick.'

'That's a good sign.' He smiled, thinking of the poor woman he had just left. She would probably be glad of a little morning sickness. 'Have you had anything to eat?'

'Couldn't stomach anything.'

'Eat one of these. You need to help your blood sugar.' He passed her a tin of chocolates that had been donated to the department by a grateful patient's family.

Leah rummaged in the tin and picked one that had bits of mint crisp in it, then popped it into her mouth, chewing reluctantly. 'This tastes like ash.'

He nodded sympathetically. He wanted to stay and talk to her, but his patient's needs had to come first right now, and Amy was worrying, and he hoped he could allay those worries with a scan.

'I need to get the portable ultrasound.'

'What do you have?'

He was reluctant to say. Did he really want to mix Leah up with a patient who might be about to lose her baby?

'Abdominal pain.'

She looked at him, assessing. 'Oh? What do you suspect?'

He sighed. 'Ovarian torsion, maybe? Ectopic? I think I've ruled out appendix.'

He saw sadness and empathy fill her face and she nodded. 'Oh… She must be scared.'

'Yeah. Look, I'd better get on…'

'Of course.'

He walked away, collected the ultrasound and went back to the cubicle, his patient Amy and her mother.

'I'm going to squirt some gel onto your belly. It'll be cold, but it will help us get a better picture.'

Ben used the probe, gliding it over Amy's skin to get as good a picture as he needed of her insides, in order to see what was going on. It was difficult. Amy kept moving and groaning with the pain.

He frowned as he stared at the screen. 'Amy, do you know you only have one fallopian tube?'

'Yes. I lost the other one to an ectopic pregnancy.'

Damn. Ben swirled the probe this way…that.

He angled the screen so that his patient could see. 'Amy, it looks like another.'

Her eyes widened. 'What? *No!* That can't be possible! Look again!'

He shook his head and showed her the empty womb. 'There's no foetus in your womb—it's growing here, in your remaining fallopian tube. We can't save this pregnancy, and it's most likely you'll lose this tube, too.'

'Lose the baby?' Amy began to cry, covering her face with her hands as she sobbed.

Hearing the pain in her cries and seeing her intense emotion made him feel awful. He tried his hardest to remain detached, but all he could think of was what if he were in the same situation soon with Leah? He knew how much she wanted to be a mother, and though her pregnancy was a mistake he knew she was hoping for a miracle. Just like Amy had been. Would he be strong enough to witness Leah's breakdown?

Amy's mother began to cry with her, trying to comfort her daughter but completely at a loss.

This was the part of doctoring Ben hated. Delivering bad news. Most of the time he had a great job. Healing people. Fixing them. Seeing them walk out through the double doors of A&E much better than when they'd walked in. But then there were days like this. Moments when nothing he said could make anything better.

He noticed she had unnatural narrowing of her fallopian tube at one end and wondered if the other one had been the same. But the knowledge wouldn't help her now. Wouldn't ward off the upset.

Amy's mother turned to him. 'This was her last chance.'

'I'm so sorry.' Ben shook his head. 'We'll need to book your daughter in for surgery. I'll give you both a moment alone, but I'll be back soon in case you have any questions.'

To see such need humbled him. To see such a drive to have a child… It was something he'd never had himself. Stories like Amy's were upsetting, but he'd always been able to separate himself from them and keep an emotional distance.

How would I feel if Leah lost our baby?

He felt something deep inside. Something stirred. What was it? He dug and dug and dug, striving to define the feeling, and when he realised what it was he discovered something about himself.

The feeling was fear. And sorrow.

He would be *sad* if she lost the baby.

He really didn't want it to happen!

How quickly thoughts could change…

CHAPTER EIGHT

'NERVOUS?' BEN COULDN'T help but notice that Leah's left leg was bouncing up and down in an anxious jitter. This was what they had been waiting for. The scan that would tell them what they wanted to know. Hopefully.

He found it odd that, considering a few months ago he'd never dreamt of being a father, here he was hoping that the baby had implanted in a *good* place in the womb, so that it would survive and have a chance to develop and grow. Live a normal life. And give him and Leah the chance to parent.

It still terrified him, but what was stronger was the realisation that he could do it.

'Having kittens. You?'

'Sweatier than a nun in a—'

'Dr Leah Hudson?' called a voice, interrupting him.

Leah raised an eyebrow. 'Than a nun in a what?'

He passed her bag, thinking fast. 'In a sauna.' He winked. 'What did you think I was going to say?'

She gave him a nervous smile and they walked towards the woman who had called Leah's name.

The ultrasound room was quite small. There was enough room for the equipment, a bed, a small sink area and a couple of chairs.

Leah was thirteen weeks and two days pregnant, and

he'd spent the last few weeks veering wildly between wondering just what the hell being an actual father might be like and worrying about how he'd feel if she miscarried.

Only now he knew. He'd be upset.

But Leah's womb had retained the pregnancy so far and here they were. In a situation he could never have imagined himself just a few short months ago. But he was an honourable man and he was ready to step up and take responsibility. Do the right thing. It was something he was used to.

He'd spent so long telling himself he didn't want to be a father that now it was going to happen he felt strangely at peace with himself. Why was that? Was it because this was happening with Leah?

She was amazing. Kind. Loving. Warm.

Brave.

He knew how terrified she was, and yet she had remained the epitome of grace and gentility, and watching her now, as she lay down on the bed and raised her shirt for the sonographer to apply gel, she glanced at him and smiled, reaching for his hand.

He gave it gladly, smiling back. Squeezing her fingers in a gesture that said, *I'm here. I'm not going anywhere.*

The smile he got in return stirred his heart, and he realised there and then that what had begun as a one-night stand had become so much more. In, oh, so many ways. And now he was determined to be there for her—refused to abandon her the way her own parents had. They were in this together.

Briefly, Ben's mind flashed back to the patient who had lost her second ectopic pregnancy and he suddenly felt guilty that he was sitting here, going through this, and she wasn't. How life played with them all. Giving to those who didn't expect it and taking away from those who wanted it more than anything.

But he wanted it now.

'You okay?' Leah whispered.

He smiled, loving the fact that she was worried about *him* at this moment. This moment that she had hoped and prayed for for many years. The moment she wanted to cherish more than any other. The first glimpse of her baby, her very own flesh and blood. There was no way of knowing yet whether the outcome was going to be positive or negative—and yet she was making sure that *he* was all right.

That was what he loved about her.

'I'm good. Look.' He saw the screen come to life as the transducer was applied to her abdomen.

The screen was filled with grey and black shapes, blurry and undefined, and then there…suddenly…was his child.

Their child.

It was too soon to know if it was a boy or a girl, a son or a daughter, but that was his child. His baby. Curled up like a minute kidney bean, the small fluttering in its chest showing a clear heartbeat.

'Oh, my God…' they both said, in awe.

He'd never felt anything like it. This moment. This precious moment in which time seemed to stop and all other sound disappeared as the sonographer turned up the volume and they heard it. The baby's heart.

Boom-boom, boom-boom, boom-boom.

Tears stung the backs of his eyes and when Leah turned to look at him, tears already streaming down her face, he lifted her hand in his and kissed the back of it.

'Ben! That's our *baby*!'

'It is! I see it.'

She clutched his hand tight and they watched and smiled as the sonographer led them through the scan, checking measurements—thigh bone, head to rump length, nuchal fold. All the measurements that had to be taken to make sure their baby was growing at the correct rate and would be healthy.

'Baby's perfect for gestation,' the sonographer said. 'Shall I print you some pictures?'

'Yes, please!' answered Ben.

He met Leah's gaze and smiled. It was real now. He'd seen it. The baby. It wasn't just a thing, the situation they talked about. It wasn't just cravings, or morning sickness, or Leah getting tired at work. It was real. A head, a heart, arms and legs, hands and feet. Growing and getting bigger within Leah. Something they had made together. A real person!

'What's the position? Is it safe?' asked Leah.

Ben sucked in a deep breath as he waited for the sonographer to give them their answer.

They sat stunned into silence on the sofa of her flat.

'I need to call Sally.'

Ben nodded. 'Of course. She'll be nervous for you.'

Leah bit her lip and looked away. 'I haven't told her yet.'

'What? She doesn't *know*? About anything?'

'She doesn't even know that I'm pregnant.'

'But I thought she was your best friend? She's carrying your child.'

'That's exactly why!'

How could she explain to him that she was scared? Guilty?

'I couldn't tell her. She thought she'd finished having kids—told me that part of her life was over—and then, when she found out about me and my difficulties, she stepped right up. Offered me her womb. Said she'd be proud to do it because I couldn't.'

'And now you're pregnant yourself.'

'And it's implanted low down in my womb. I have a chance to carry my own child! To bring it to term and give birth! It's what I've always wanted, and yet I've put Sally through pregnancy again. Do you know how sick she got? And she's already getting stretch marks!'

She could feel tears burning her eyes. This happened a lot just lately. Every time she thought about what she was putting her best friend through.

'She loves you. She'll understand.'

Leah nodded. 'I know. But I feel like I've lied. I worry that she'll think I won't want the baby that she's carrying. I'm putting her through labour and birth—something she swore she'd never do again, because last time she got a third-degree tear and complications afterwards. But she stepped up anyway, because she thought I couldn't do this, and now that I can she needs to know.'

Ben made them both a drink and they sat on the couch together, looking at the scan photos.

'How do you feel?' she asked him.

'It feels…weird.'

'How so?'

Weird enough to run away? Weird enough to dump her? She hoped not, but that was what she was used to. And she'd been warned about Ben, about how he'd broken a few hearts at the hospital already. She almost couldn't believe they were talking about the same person, because the Ben *she* knew seemed nothing like the Ben who was gossiped about.

'Like I'm standing in the eye of a storm and all these

thoughts and feelings are whirling around me, faster and faster, and I don't know which one to focus on first.'

She grimaced. 'That bad, huh?'

'No, it's not bad. It's just…scary.'

'Need-to-run-away scary, or a-little-bit-apprehensive scary?'

Ben put down his drink and took her hands in his. 'I'm not running away. Hey…' He used a finger to lift her chin and make her look at him. 'It's all going to be okay. *We're* going to be okay.'

It felt good to be this close to him again. Side by side, faces close, looking into each other's eyes. What did she want to see in those eyes of his? Certainty? Reliability? Dependability? She wanted to feel that he would be there for her. Would always look out for her. Was that asking too much? Was that hoping for too much happiness? Was that even a *thing*?

But there was something else in his gaze too. There was attraction and desire—the things she still felt the pull of herself, despite having worked so hard to keep Ben in the 'friend zone' for so many weeks now…

Leah's gaze dropped uncertainly to his mouth. 'Are you going to kiss me?' she whispered.

'I'd like to.'

'Only kiss me?'

He smiled wickedly. 'And more besides…'

She closed her eyes as his lips met hers and allowed everything else that was happening to just float away, untethered and unhindered. All that mattered right now was the feel of his lips against her own. The warmth of his hands upon her face, the gentleness with which he touched her.

When he broke away to look at her, to see if she wanted more than this, she reached out and pulled him close.

Yes. I want more.

The intensity of the kiss deepened and she felt her body awaken in anticipation. She knew this man's touch. What it was capable of. And she wanted all of it. The feeling of him. The warmth of him. His desire.

This was no one-night stand, like it had been before. This wasn't just lust and hitting the peaks. This was intimacy and knowing him more than she had known him before. He wasn't a stranger. This was a man she liked. This was a man she cared for. This was the man who had fathered the baby within her womb. There was a connection. Something stronger than two strangers.

She felt for the buttons of his shirt, undoing them, pulling at the material, eager to feel his skin beneath her fingertips. She could already feel heat and muscle and sinew and she needed more. Needed to feel all of him. To breathe him in. To know him once again now that their bond was stronger than before.

Ben undid his belt, then helped her off with her top. Her skin felt alive with his touch. She wanted his hands on her, stroking her, touching her, teasing nerve endings that were electric.

And suddenly she was lying back, naked, his body atop her, his long, lean length stretched out across the fullness of her, and it was one of the most delicious feelings in the world. And then, slowly, he began to trail his lips down her neck, licking the dip at the base of her throat, kissing her, tasting her, until he was holding her hips and his lips were over the skin below her belly button. Here he paused, as if considering what lay beneath.

He licked once. Kissed her skin, her gently rounded

abdomen, gazing upon her belly as if it held precious treasure that hypnotised him.

'Ben?'

'Yes?'

'You won't hurt me.'

He looked up at her and met her flustered gaze before proceeding to drop his head lower.

She'd meant to say he wouldn't hurt the baby, assuming that was what he was worrying about, but had she meant something else? Had she been asking him a question? Or making a statement?

But she didn't have too long to consider that as his tongue expertly got to work. Her back arched away from the couch and she gasped for air as Ben sent her soaring to the heavens.

When she opened her eyes his face was next to hers, and his mouth claimed her as his hardness pressed against her, teasingly close.

'Ben…' she breathed, urging him on, and he plunged into her.

She gasped, clutching him to her. She was lost. Lost in a world of passion and desire and need. A need to envelop him, to hold him close, to be taken to the heights. But this joining was more than just that. It was a redefining of their relationship. A strengthening of their bond. They had made something physical. Now they were making something emotional.

As he moved against her, lips on her neck, breathing hard as he thrust into her, she couldn't help but groan and gasp aloud. She wanted him so much! Could feel her own excitement begin to peak with every delicious, delectable thrust. She pulled him towards her harder and harder as they both climaxed, calling out, breathing heavily, pant-ing and slowing, their bodies slick with sweat, before they slowed to stillness and he kissed her again.

That heat… That tingle where their bodies were still as one…

Leah smiled, then began to chuckle. 'Oh, my God… Wow.'

Ben propped himself up on one elbow and looked down at her, kissing her once more. He stared deeply into her eyes. What was he looking for? What did he hope to see in her face?

Leah stroked his face. 'We do like complicated, don't we?'

He smiled and raised an eyebrow. 'I guess we do. Want to get complicated again?'

She laughed. 'Really? Again?'

'Why not? But it might be nice to move somewhere a little comfier.'

'The bedroom?'

He pretended to look as if he was thinking about it. Then, 'I do believe that worked once before, so why not?'

And he stood up and scooped her into his arms as if she was as light as a feather, and they both laughed as he carried her into her bedroom and lay her down upon the sheets.

CHAPTER NINE

'LEAH? THERE'S A lady here to see you,' said Richard, poking his head through the cubicle curtains.

'Who is it?' she asked as she applied the last sterile strip to her patient's wound.

'Er... I think she said her name was Sally Lombard?' *Sally!*

Leah had called her that morning after Ben had left, wanting some privacy to make the call. She'd felt very nervous about calling her friend, and then Sally had been out and she'd had to leave a message, saying she needed to speak to her in person so she'd call again later.

She hadn't expected Sally to turn up at her work!

Still, it was nice, and Leah was due her lunch break, so it would give them the opportunity they needed to talk.

Her patient hobbled out of the cubicle on crutches, and with a set of instructions on how to take care of his wound, and Leah hurried off to write up her notes. She would only have an hour for lunch and she didn't want to waste it.

Ben was at the doctors' desk, just coming off the phone, when she arrived.

'Hey, are you free for lunch?' she asked.

He checked his watch. 'I can be. You want to grab a bite somewhere special?'

'No, no. It's just that…well, Sally's here and I need to tell her about the baby, and I thought it might be a good idea if you could join us later and she could meet you.'

She saw him hesitate.

'Your surrogate?'

'Yes.'

'Sure. What time do you want me to interrupt?'

'About one-thirty—in the cafeteria? That should give me time to tell her the basics.'

'Perfect. I'll see you then.' He got up and walked away, leaving her watching him go.

Leah quickly filled in her notes and filed the patient's record, and then headed off to find Sally, who was sitting in the waiting room with all the patients.

'Sal!'

Her best friend looked wonderful! Swollen-bellied and amazing. After she'd given her friend a hug and a kiss she took a moment to lay her hand on Sally's belly and felt her baby give a strong kick in response.

'You're looking good. And this one is growing so fast!'

'It sure is. It's a kick-ass, like it's mama. I swear it's taken up kick-boxing in there. My bladder is being used as a punch bag.'

Leah couldn't help but smile. She'd been speaking to Sally often on the phone, but they hadn't seen each other for a month or two and the physical difference in her friend was astounding. And to think that soon she too would look this big. If not bigger!

'The hospital has a cafeteria that sells pretty decent food, if you're up for it?'

'Always starving with this one inside me. I can't remember getting this hungry carrying my own kids.'

Leah threaded her arm through Sally's and they waited for a lift to take them up to the cafeteria floor. Before long they were choosing food from the long display and settling down in a small booth.

'So, how are you? How have you been?' asked Sally. 'I've missed seeing you, but it's been so hectic at home. Andrew's rehearsing for his role in the school play and I've been helping out, making the sets for the drama department. I swear, if I hear another speech from *Hamlet* I'm going to go crazy!'

'Andrew's playing Hamlet? That's brilliant news!'

'Well, he's very dramatic—as you very well know. The theatre is in his blood, darling!' She sipped at her decaf cappuccino. 'But enough about him—tell me what's going on with you. What's this big news you want to tell me?' Sally leaned in, grinning. 'Have you met someone?'

Leah coloured as the moment of truth came upon her. Why did she feel so guilty about telling her this? Sally was her best friend! She wouldn't be upset—she knew the turmoil Leah had been through. But this news—the pregnancy—somehow felt like a sort of betrayal and she didn't know why.

'I have met someone, yes.'

Sally's eyes widened in glee and she squealed. 'Really? What? Here? Who is he? What's he like?'

'His name's Ben. Ben Willoughby. He's a doctor.'

'Willoughby? Like from *Sense and Sensibility*? Tell me you fell over in the rain and he rescued you on his white steed? Oh! This is so *exciting*!'

Leah sipped at her orange juice and smiled nervously. 'Not quite. I didn't know he was a doctor when I met him. He's that guy I told you about. The one-night stand?' She blushed.

'Your hot stud is your new beau?'

Leah flushed. 'Yes.' Then she giggled. *Nerves*.

Why, oh, why had they left it so long to talk like this?

It had been ages! She'd missed chatting with Sally. But guilt had kept her away, and talking on the phone had seemed easier, because Sally wouldn't see the lies on Leah's face.

'I've asked him to join us in a minute because I want you to meet him.'

Sally looked at her in surprise. 'So it's serious, then?'

'Yes. At least I think so.'

'You *think* so?'

'Well, it's complicated…'

Sally pointed at her own stomach. 'You mean this complication?'

'Kind of…'

'What do you mean? Have you told him about the baby? Oh, please tell me you've been honest with the guy, Leah! He needs to know before he walks in here and sees this belly of mine!'

'He knows. I've told him. But that's not the complication I wanted to mention.'

Her friend frowned. 'Why? What else is going on?'

Leah let out a big sigh, not sure how to say it. Just come straight out with it? Just blurt it out? Or gently sow the seeds?

'Our one-night stand… Well, it kind of led to something more than just a relationship.'

'He gave you an STD?' Sally whispered, shock peppering her voice.

'No!' Leah felt her face colour again. 'But he did give me something.'

Sally frowned, waiting.

It was so hard to say the words. But they needed to be said. 'I'm pregnant, Sal. I'm carrying a baby.'

Sally sat back, stunned, her face a picture of total shock and disbelief. Her lower jaw moved as if she were trying to formulate words, questions to ask, but no sounds came out.

Leah reached over and grabbed her friend's hand. 'I'm just over three months pregnant.'

Sally continued to look at her, open-mouthed, her hand resting protectively over her belly. Eventually she managed to find the power of speech. 'But…how? I didn't think… You said that…'

'The usual way.'

'But what about…?'

Leah shook her head. 'I don't know. I didn't think it was possible. But it happened, and I've had a scan and…' She reached into her bag and pulled out her scan picture. 'And the baby has implanted in a good place. I might be able to carry to term! It has a good chance of surviving!'

Sally picked up the scan picture and stared at it. 'Leah, this is like a miracle! How do you feel?'

'Terrified! But…happy.'

Then her friend frowned. 'And do you still want…?' She rubbed at her own swollen abdomen, unable to finish the sentence.

'Of course I do! Don't even *think* that.'

At that moment Leah saw Ben walk into the cafeteria. She gave him a little wave.

'Here he comes.'

Sally looked around and saw him. She turned back to her friend, blushing madly. 'That's *him*? Bloody hell, Leah…'

Leah couldn't help but smile as Ben approached.

'Hi. You must be Sally. I'm Ben.'

'Pleased to meet you.'

'Have you…er…?' He looked down at Leah.

'Yes, I've told her.'

Ben nodded. 'Good. That's good. And how is everything?' He slid into a seat next to her.

'Good!'

They all looked at each other, unsure what to say next.

'Well, this is a huge surprise...' said Sally.

Leah frowned. 'You don't mind?'

Sally looked surprised. 'Why would I mind?'

Leah shrugged. 'Because I'm putting you through a pregnancy that you never wanted?'

Sally waved her hands in dismissal. 'That's ridiculous! You could never have foreseen this happening! This is a *wonderful* miracle, Leah. You're going to have two babies!' She beamed a smile and glanced at Ben. 'How do *you* feel about that?'

Ben looked at Leah and took her hand in his. 'I'm happy about it. It's a shock, but it's something we're determined to tackle together.'

Sally nodded. 'Okay. It's a lot to take in, isn't it?' She took another look at the scan picture on the table and smiled.

Leah sat biting the skin around her nails. She'd been doing that a lot lately. Her mind was running through a thousand thoughts—worrying about being in her second trimester, worrying about whether the scan really had been as accurate as they were hoping it was, terrified that somehow the sonographer had got it wrong and that each day was just a ticking of the time-bomb until the day her body failed her.

Because that was what she'd always believed. That the one thing she was supposed to be able to do as a woman—carry a child—was not a choice for her. Her womb had developed badly...it wasn't strong enough.

But now she'd been told she was lucky, That one in a million chance…

'Dr Hudson? We need you.' Richard stood beside her.

She looked up absently. What is it?'

'Nail gun injury.'

She got up, sighing. 'Okay. I'm coming.'

I guess a bit of blood and gore might take my mind off the mess that I'm in.

She knew it was time to tell everyone in the department that she was pregnant. Or should she wait? Until she really began to show? When she felt safer about carrying this baby to term? She'd read an article online the other day, about the dangers of carrying a child with a bicornuate uterus, and even some of the success stories had still seemed pretty scary.

She followed Richard through to her patient, who lay on a hospital bed, his modesty covered by a blanket, on his stomach. There was a strange peak in the blanket over the crest of his gluteus maximus.

'How did you get shot in the bottom with a nail gun?'

Her patient coloured. 'It was an accident.'

She lifted up the blanket. The nail had pierced the flesh of the man's gluteus maximus and still stuck out from his right buttock. A small trickle of blood had crept down his thigh.

Leah didn't think it had pierced anything vital. If anything, he'd need a plaster and maybe a tetanus shot.

'We're doing a garage conversion. My parents are moving in with us and we decided to make them an annexe, so they can be independent. We were in there… working.'

'And how did you get shot?'

The patient's wife answered. 'Martin told me he'd been meeting up with his ex-wife.'

Leah raised an eyebrow. '"Meeting up"?'

'Yeah. It's his code for sex. He gets all the fun of play-ing off two women and I get my in-laws moving in. Not exactly a fair trade, is it? So I shot him when he bent over to pick up a two-by-four. It was kinda fun, seeing him fall flat on his face.' She smiled maliciously down at him, hatred filling her face. 'Cheating swine!'

'Hey! I didn't—'

Leah held up her hand for silence. 'This constitutes assault—'

'Hey, I'm the victim here!' the patient's wife stated, leaning forward, her hands on the bed. 'He just got what he deserved!'

'You can't go around assaulting people. Especially with nail guns. They're dangerous. You could have caused him some serious damage.'

'But I didn't! All he's gonna suffer from is a painful backside every time he sits down and a bruised ego. I could have done a lot worse!'

'I'm not gonna press charges…' Martin mumbled.

'Are you going to see your ex-wife again?' she de-manded.

He looked up at his current wife and shook his head.

His wife smiled. 'Good. You'd better not. Because if you do there'll be hell to pay.'

Leah gave Martin a shot of local anaesthetic and re-moved the nail. It came out quite easily and she cleaned the wound, then put in a single stitch. She gave Martin a tetanus shot and told him to see his doctor in about five days to make sure he was healing properly.

He pulled up his trousers, looking sheepish, and left with his wife.

Leah watched them go. Were some people just prone to having bad stuff happen to them? Because so far she felt as if she'd had her fair share, and she was not content to roll over and let more bad stuff happen.

She knew she had to fight for her happiness.

For her baby and for her future with Ben.

Leah was stepping out of the shower, adjusting a towel around her hair, when she heard the doorbell ring.

She turned down the small corridor that led to her front door and recognised the silhouette of Ben through the glass. He was ringing the bell again.

She opened the door. 'Hey.'

His gaze travelled up and down her towel-clad body before returning to her face. 'Hi.'

'Come on in.' She stepped back. 'Do you want tea or coffee?'

'Whatever you're having.'

She smiled. 'Apple juice it is, then. I can't stomach hot drinks at the moment.'

She fetched their drinks and then settled down next to him on the couch, snuggling into his embrace.

'I wasn't expecting you to come round tonight.'

'I never got the chance to really speak to you today—we were rushed off our feet.'

'We certainly were. What do you fancy doing?'

He raised an eyebrow. 'Well, I was going to suggest we went out for dinner, but your towelling outfit is rather distracting and now I'm thinking of something else entirely.' He smiled and pulled her towards him, kissing her on the lips.

She laughed. 'I bet you are! And although that sounds very tempting indeed...' She ran her finger down the front of his chest, knowing exactly how much fun that 'something else' would be, then looked up to meet his gaze. 'I'm starving and dinner sounds great. It'll be like a real date! And we can have dessert afterwards.'

She smiled at him, letting him know exactly what kind of dessert she was referring to.

He smiled back. 'Are you sure we can't have dessert first?'

'You look gorgeous.'

Leah blushed as she stood in the doorway of her bedroom, wearing a dress that hadn't seen the light of day since before she'd graduated. In fact, she was amazed she could still fit into it. It was a rich electric blue wrap dress that clung to her body, and she had to admit to herself that she felt good wearing it.

'Thanks. Where are we going for dinner?'

'I know a great little place called Verdant. Have you ever been there?'

She shook her head.

'It's plant-based cooking and the chef is amazing. You'll love it! But first there's one thing I have to do.'

'What's that?' She looked up at him, curious.

He cupped her face and brought her lips to his, kissing her tenderly and making her feel as if her insides were melting. 'That.'

She smiled at him. 'An aperitif?'

'Something to hold back the hunger.'

His eyes gazed down at her with such need that she almost suggested they didn't go out to eat at all!

But her absolute hunger—caused, no doubt, by her pregnancy—forced her to create a priority and her belly won out. 'Let's go before I change my mind. Or before I end up eating *you*.'

He smiled. 'Don't tempt me.'

She took his hand and led him out through the front

door, laughing at his groan of frustration as she headed out towards his car, parked in front.

He opened her door for her and then walked round to the other side and got in. 'Our first official date.'

She laughed. 'Yep! We've done all this back to front.'

He raised an eyebrow. 'Any regrets?'

'No!'

Absolutely not. Not any more. She was still scared. Who wouldn't be? But did she regret the situation? No. No way. Ben had given her her dream and she was so lucky to have him at her side.

CHAPTER TEN

LEAH LOOKED UP at the clock on the wall. Ben was late. He should have been here ten minutes ago! Where was he? Stuck in traffic? If so, why hadn't he texted or called?

Life was going quite well for them recently. Ben quite clearly making an effort to date her. Woo her. One day he'd brought her flowers, another he'd come to the flat and cooked her a proper meal, to make sure she was eating well. They'd even gone out to see a show at the theatre— an old Agatha Christie mystery.

He'd walked her home afterwards, and when they'd got to the doorstep she'd asked him if he wanted to come in and stay the night.

'I can't.' He'd sighed, leaning in towards her and inhaling the scent of her perfume from her neck. 'I have an early start tomorrow, and if I stay I won't want to get out of your bed.'

She'd smiled, closing her eyes in bliss at the feel of his hot breath on her neck, his fingers in her hair, the delicious sensation of his teeth nibbling at her earlobe. 'Are you sure?' Her hands had swept under the edges of his jacket and she'd been able to feel the heat and hardness of his body next to hers. And she'd wanted him.

He'd groaned. 'No...'

He'd stayed the night. And he'd been late the next

morning. And they'd grinned at each other like idiots all day long.

That was when the word had got out. That and the fact that now she was quite clearly pregnant, rather than just losing the battle against the sweets she kept on eating.

Gossip had ricocheted around the department like a pinball, but it hadn't actually been as bad as she'd expected.

'Congratulations!' Richard had said, giving her a hug. 'If he ever drops the ball, then give me a shout.'

She'd laughed. 'I will.'

'I'm so pleased for you!'

'I hope you'll both be very happy!'

'You make a great couple!'

There were one or two doubters. She'd been treating a patient in a cubicle one day when she'd heard two HCAs talking quietly near the sluice.

'Can you imagine getting pregnant by *him*? He's hot, but he's not exactly the commitment type, is he?'

'No. I bet he's got loads of kids he doesn't even know about.'

The comments had hurt, but she'd chosen not to say anything. She knew the truth of Ben's feelings, and she was the only one who knew the battles he'd been fighting. Ben might have played the field before, but he'd been careful. And he hadn't slept with *every* woman he'd spent time with. Sometimes he'd only wanted the pleasure of their company, not their bed. That wasn't what it had been about.

But she hadn't said that to *them*. It was none of their business. *She* knew how it was for both of them and that was what mattered.

Now Leah shifted in her seat, trying to get comfortable. She was five months pregnant, and awaiting her second and final scan. Everything was moving so fast. She'd thought they had loads of time ahead of them to be a couple, for it to just be the two of them, but now Sally was nearing her due date and she herself felt huge!

Five months already, and the time was flying by...

She wanted Ben to be here because today they were going to discover the sex of their baby and find out more about its positioning, check that its growth was as expected.

Once upon a time she'd thought she'd never get this far with a baby and yet here she was. With a nice round abdomen she could stroke. And when her baby decided to stretch she'd often lift up her top to watch her belly undulate and move. It was a miracle.

Last night she and Ben had sat on the sofa discussing things.

'What do you want? A girl or a boy?' she'd asked.

He'd shrugged. 'I don't mind.'

'Well, which is easier to look after?'

He'd let out a sigh. 'They both have their pros and cons...'

She'd laughed and swiped at his arm.

And now he was late.

And she didn't want to find out on her own.

'Dr Leah Hudson?'

Oh, shoot.

She got up and walked over to the sonographer. 'I'm waiting for my partner. He should be here any minute.'

'Well, we'll get started and he can join us when he gets here. We're already running behind.'

'Of course. Sorry.' She hopped up onto the couch and lay down, adjusting her waistband so the sonographer could apply a paper towel and then the cold gel.

She was feeling apprehensive and excited at the same

time—but also a little lonely. She hadn't realised before just how much it meant to her to have him with her for this. To be in a relationship. To have someone to lean on. Ben was steady and sure, despite his fears about being a father, and he'd never given her any reason to doubt him.

Imagine if I was going through all this on my own...

Tears threatened at the backs of her eyes, but just as she thought she might start bawling her eyes out because she *was* on her own there was a small knock on the door and Ben was there.

'You're late!'

She felt her bottom jaw wobble and then that was that. She was crying. Her emotions were a giant rollercoaster that she wasn't prepared for. Today was so important! Terrifying. Despite the reassurances of the previous scan, she still felt that she needed him—just in case.

'I'm so sorry! There was a traffic accident and I stopped to give assistance. When I tried to ring you my phone had died and I couldn't get through.'

'I thought you'd forgotten me! I don't know why I'm crying!'

The sonographer smiled at her and passed her a tissue.

'How could I forget you?' He grabbed hold of her shaking hand and squeezed it tight, then kissed the back of her hand. 'Okay, what did I miss?'

'We were just about to start.'

Leah sniffed and wiped her nose and turned hungrily to the screen.

The sonographer did her thing. Measured thigh length and head-to-rump length and checked the butterfly patterning of the brain. She checked the amniotic fluid, counted the vessels in the umbilical cord, fingers and toes, and then she allowed them to hear the heartbeat.

'It's perfect,' she said.

'Baby's okay?'

'Baby seems fine. Do you want to know the sex?'

'Yes, please.'

She positioned the transducer so that they could clearly see what they were having.

Leah turned to smile at Ben. 'We're having a boy!' She felt tears of joy spring from her eyes and began to sob happy tears. 'A son! I can't believe it!'

And then the sonographer began to frown.

It had been a truly heart-stopping moment. Finding out he was going to have a son. Someone who would carry on his name. Someone he'd truly have to be a role model to. Of course he'd be a great role model for a girl, too. Show her how men were meant to treat women, with respect. But having a son...that meant so much!

He'd covered his mouth with his hand, quite unable to believe it, and had felt as if he might punch the air in celebration. But then the sonographer had leaned in towards her monitor and begun to frown.

'What is it?' he'd asked.

The sonographer had turned the screen so he could see more clearly.

'The placenta. It's lying over the opening of the cervix. We'll need to keep an eye on this. It's placenta praevia. Normally it would lie near the top of the uterus, but due to Leah's shape it's down here—quite low.'

'Will it move?'

'It might. I can't say for sure. Sometimes a placenta can move as the uterus enlarges, but due to the bicornuate shape of your wife's uterus this may not happen.'

He hadn't corrected her when she'd said *'your wife'*. There were more important things to worry about.

Just when they'd thought all their worries were over.

Placenta praevia could cause problems. He knew that as an emergency doctor. He'd seen one or two cases of it in his career. Leah could be at risk of bleeding. And heavy bleeding could put Leah and the baby at serious life-threatening risk.

'You need to be aware of any bleeding that you may have. Often the bleeding can be painless, or it can occur after sexual intercourse.'

He'd gripped Leah's hand in his own.

'We'll get you in for another scan at thirty-two weeks. Check its position then. If it hasn't moved we may need to admit you. We wouldn't want to have to wait if you need an emergency Caesarean.'

Leah had looked small and frightened once again. 'Okay.'

She'd had to go back to work, but he wasn't on shift until the afternoon that day and he'd found himself driving through the streets. He'd thought he'd been driving aimlessly, but he hadn't, and now he found himself pulling up outside his childhood home.

He hadn't been here for years. The last time he'd seen his parents had been… He couldn't remember. Looking at the old terraced house, with its grubby net curtains and a garden filled with weeds, he almost didn't go in. But something compelled him. A need for family? If that was so, why hadn't he gone to see his brother or sister? Surrounded himself with happy childish laughter and naughty nephews and nieces?

He needed to see his parents. Needed to tell them they were going to be grandparents. Despite everything, he felt he still needed to tell them that.

Inside, everything was at it usually was—Mum sat on the couch reading a magazine, with a cigarette dying in her fingers, and Dad was gazing at the television, one leg over the arm of his chair.

'Ben! What are you doing here? We don't normally warrant a visit,' said his mother.

He nodded, nervous, and sat down on the edge of a seat. 'I...er... I thought I'd pop in and see how you were both doing.'

They hadn't moved on. It was all the same. The wallpaper on the walls was the same chintzy design he'd grown up with. The couch was still part of the old brown suite, just a little more worn. The rug in front of the fire, now bald of the tassels around its edge, was dull and flat. A thick fug of cigarette smoke hung in the air.

'We're doing all right. How's it going at that fancy hospital of yours?'

They'd always thought he was a bit above himself, wanting to be a doctor. 'Yeah, good. We're busy. Very busy.'

'Yeah, we see it on the news! All those poor people waiting to be seen—and no wonder! You aren't there— you're out visiting your folks.' His mum laughed and sucked at her cigarette, coughing afterwards.

'I'll be there later.'

'Something up? You look a bit...worried.'

She's noticed? Well, wonders will never cease.

'There is something I'd like to talk to you both about.'

His dad muted the television and turned around. 'You met a girl at last? What's her name? She up the duff?'

Ben smiled politely. He wasn't used to sharing things with his parents. And he'd never liked the way they could be so crass. No wonder he'd been so keen to leave. He had nothing in common with them. But, as the saying went, you couldn't choose your family, and despite all the wrong they had done they were still his family.

'Her name's Leah. She's another doctor in my department.'

'Leah? Sounds posh,' his mum said.

'She's nice. She's perfect.'

'Is it serious, then?'

He nodded. 'Yes. And you're right, Dad. I'm going to be a father.'

'We're going to be grandparents again? I'm too young for so many grandkids!'

Ben smiled politely again, determined not to be rattled. He hadn't expected thrilled enthusiasm, but he had hoped for maybe some congratulations. He should have known they'd be selfish about it.

'Are you going to marry her?' his dad asked. 'Because you want to think about that before you do. Your mum trapped *me*, you know.'

'I never trapped you, you old sod!'

The argument began in earnest and Ben sat there, listening to the same old story he'd heard time and time again. How his dad's life might have been different if he hadn't been saddled with a load of kids. How his mum thought that if he'd had enough self-control to keep it in his trousers then neither of them would have ended up where they were. Each blamed the other, each utterly committed to the roles they had carved out for themselves, practised and rehearsed over many years.

Ben stood up and went to the door. 'I just thought you ought to know you're having a grandson. But don't worry—I won't expect you to babysit.'

And he closed the door behind him and left, stepping out into clean fresh air and sucking it into his lungs in an attempt to purify himself of his visit.

Why had he gone back? Out of some vain hope that something might have changed? That a new grandchild, something that most parents yearned for, might be a catalyst for change? Might make them see something other than themselves?

I should have known better.

Well. He'd done his duty. He'd informed them and they weren't bothered and he wasn't going to let their negativity have any impact on his son's life.

My son's life.

It felt good to think about that. His first duty of protecting his child. Of course there was the placenta issue to worry about, but there was nothing he could do about that.

Ben got into the car and drove towards the hospital. He wasn't due there for another couple of hours, but he suddenly felt the need to see Leah and just hold her in his arms.

His past was his past.

She was his future.

Leah and the baby.

His *son.*

'Hey, what's this for?' asked Leah as Ben stepped into her arms.

He sighed as he breathed in the scent of her hair. 'It's for me. Just… Let's just stand here like this for a minute.'

Leah smiled as she leaned in to his chest, listening to the steady beat of his heart as he held her tightly. How could she be so lucky? To have this man by her side?

He'd turned up at work a little earlier than she'd expected, though. Was it because of this morning? The scan? Finding out their baby was a boy? About the placenta praevia?

She'd been worrying, too. But, like the shape of her uterus, she knew deep down that there was nothing she could do about it but hope.

Perhaps he'd come to the same conclusion and was feeling a little powerless? But she wasn't going to complain about being in his arms. Being in Ben's arms felt wonderful! He made her feel safe when he held her like this. Cherished and loved.

Not that he'd told her that he loved her, or she him. It was probably a bit too soon for that—they both had so much going on in their lives. But their feelings were growing in the right direction and that was what mattered.

He kissed the top of her head and let her go.

'You okay?' she asked.

He nodded, smiling. 'I am now.'

She stroked his arm. 'Big day, huh?'

'Yeah.'

'We'll be okay. We can do this, you and me.'

'Yes. Yes, we can.'

Arty Miller had an open fracture of his tibia and fibula. The result of a challenging walk up a hillside with his three boys. According to Arty, they had come across an outcrop of rocks where they had decided to stop and partake of a small picnic. After they'd eaten they'd all started clambering on the rocks and seeing who could jump from the highest point.

'And, me being me, I had to show them, didn't I? That I could jump from the highest point. And I don't know... I landed funny. I felt something snap and that was that...'

Arty had been in fine fettle throughout his helicopter flight, according to the air ambulance doctor, and his sons had been brought in by road. A little cold...a little scared.

Leah and Ben were trying to keep them all feeling chipper until the boys' mum arrived to look after them.

'Do you go on adventurous walks a lot, then?' she asked.

'Every weekend, if we can. I like to get them away from their screens and it's a good bonding experience for them all—especially since we got Luke about six months ago.'

Luke smiled. Clearly he was the youngest of the three boys, aged around nine.

'You foster?' asked Ben.

'No, we've adopted. All of them, in fact. Dante was first, then we got Hugo, and finally Luke.' Arty beamed a smile at all his boys, obviously as proud as could be. 'Though I think our family is done now—and I'm sure my wife will agree when she gets here.'

Leah smiled at Arty and then looked to Ben to see what he thought.

Ben was looking at Arty in obvious awe. 'Wow. That's amazing.'

'Fliss and I were travel journalists. I met her in a jungle camp in Borneo, would you believe? We spent all our time flitting our way around the world—it was something we both loved. But then we got married, decided to settle down, and babies just didn't happen so we decided to adopt.' He smiled, ruffling the hair of Dante, who stood closest to him. 'Best thing we ever did, getting these three.'

Leah smiled at them all. 'Sounds amazing. We need more people like you guys—opening your homes and your hearts to children who need them.'

Arty nodded. 'Yes, we do. Though *you* look as if

you're growing one of your own, there! How far along are you?'

She rubbed at her belly as if only just noticing it. 'Five months.'

'Well, let me tell you something. You can travel the world and see the most beautiful sights—the Pyramids, Victoria Falls, Machu Picchu—but nothing—*nothing*— is as wonderful as being a parent. You enjoy every moment. Not everyone is as blessed.'

Leah nodded, feeling herself welling up at his words. 'I will.'

At that moment the doors to Majors opened up and in came a small woman with frizzy, auburn hair and rosy red cheeks—Fliss.

She ran up to her kids and gave them all a hug. And then moved over to her husband and clutched his hand. 'What trouble have you got yourself into this time, huh?'

Ben explained what had happened and told Fliss they were waiting for Arty to be taken up for surgery, and that afterwards he would be moved to the adult orthopaedic ward.

When they'd gone Leah sat down at the doctors' desk with Ben and wiped her eyes with the heel of her hand. 'What a wonderful family.'

'Yeah, they are. It gives you hope, doesn't it? To see that some families get it right?'

She nodded. 'I think me and you were in the minority, you know? I like to think that our childhoods were anomalies. Especially when I see two people like Arty and Fliss, who are clearly very loving parents.' She smiled, thinking. 'I wonder what it's like? To grow up and be cherished and adored? Do you think you'd know how lucky you are? Do you think most people take that for granted?'

'Probably.'

'But at least we know it's possible. Arty took on those three children who aren't his. Three children who came to him with baggage and backstories and problems of their own. But he took them on and took them on gladly.'

'Are you trying to tell me something?' Ben smiled.

She laughed gently. 'Maybe. We haven't really talked much about the other baby. I know that you being with me will mean taking on more than your own child, and that's a big thing. But if Arty has shown us anything, it's that it can be a success, and those children mean as much to him as if they were his own flesh and blood.' She reached out and laid her hand on his. 'I'm just saying that I know what I'm asking of you.'

His thumb stroked the back of her hand. His gentle caress spoke a thousand truths as his face suddenly clouded with doubt. 'I'm going to do this, Leah. Be their father. But what if I'm not good enough? What if I'm not like Arty? What if I can't do it? Be a good example?'

'You will be—I know it. But let's just take it day by day. Hour by hour, if necessary.' She squeezed his hand. 'Remember, I don't know what I'm doing either. We can stumble blindly through all the parenting pitfalls together.'

'You paint a wonderful picture.' He smiled.

'Let's consider it our very own adventure. We might not have travelled the world, seen the Pyramids or Machu Picchu, but we both know we want to get this right. We both want these children to be loved, yes?'

He nodded. 'Yes.'

'Okay. Well, the fact that we're worrying about doing it right means that we care, and that already puts us streets ahead of our own parents.'

He smiled again.

'You know… I want to start decorating the nursery soon,' she said. 'You could come round and help me do it? Let's build a dream nest for our children. Start them off with a warm, loving home.'

He nodded, but she could see something uncertain in his eyes. Something that worried him. And she understood that. She was scared, too. No matter how brave they were pretending to be in the face of such uncertainty she was terrified, too.

This was so much to take on. Both their lives changing so drastically and unexpectedly. Especially in Ben's case. It was natural for him to have worries and concerns. All new parents did. But she felt strongly that as long as they kept talking to each other they would get through this.

And do so successfully.

Ben's next patient took him into Minors. A woman who had found a lump in her breast.

Brianna Jones was a fifty-two-year-old woman who had arrived with her partner of twenty years, Carol.

Ben performed an ultrasound, as he was unable to send her for a mammogram straight away, and found the lump in question. It was about three centimetres across, with ill-defined borders, microlobulated margins and it was spiculated, which meant that there were points and spikes on the surface of it. It certainly wasn't a diagnosis of a breast cancer—he'd need a biopsy for that—but it certainly indicated further testing.

Whilst they waited for the test results to come back, Ben looked up to find Carol standing in front of him.

'You okay?' he asked.

She nodded. 'If this is breast cancer, what does it mean?'

'Let's wait and see what the tests say before we worry about that.'

'Please... I need you to give me the worst-case scenario. I need to know what I might be dealing with.'

Ben sighed. He really didn't like giving out worst-case scenarios until he had definitive diagnoses. 'If it is cancer then we need to find out what type before we can treat it.'

Carol nodded. 'I can't lose her. She's my life. I don't know where I'd be without her.'

Ben looked across the department at Brianna, who lay back on the hospital bed, fidgeting with a tissue. 'We still don't know anything for sure. Let's wait until the test results come back and then we can make a plan.'

'In Brianna I've found a friend who knows me inside and out. Who loves me more than I ever thought possible. And that's a gift. Not many people get that chance in life and I don't want to lose mine.'

'I understand. But you're not there yet. We don't know anything. Not really.'

Carol smiled down at him. 'No. I guess not. I'm sorry. I'm just freaking out. I hate having control taken away from me and this...the possibility of cancer...well, that takes away all control, doesn't it?'

Ben nodded. 'Life has a way of throwing you curveballs when you least expect them. You've done the right thing. You've come in. We're investigating it early.'

'I already lost her once. Before. I've loved her for years, but her family put pressure on her to marry a man. It was what was expected back in the eighties. I thought my chance at happiness was gone, but I got her back. Finding the right person, who knows you, inside and out, is one of the greatest gifts we can ever give ourselves.' She turned to look at Brianna. 'I ought to get back. Thanks for talking with me. Will the results be long, do you think?'

'I'll chase them up now.'

'Thank you.' Carol headed back to Brianna's cubicle.

Ben looked down at the computer screen and thought about what Carol had said.

He had spent his entire life telling himself he didn't want to be a father and didn't want to settle down with anyone because it was all too much, because of his childhood.

He'd thought that he might have a lonely life, and had tried to fill it with fun when he could, and now all of that had changed. For the better. All he'd ever needed was the one thing he'd always run away from.

Leah was amazing—and she was carrying their son. And Leah's friend Sally was carrying another baby for Leah. And he was with Leah. And that meant he was going to be a dad to two.

Yeah, it was scary.

But if he got it right…it would be the most amazing thing in the world!

A chance to create a home and a childhood such as he'd never had, to let his children experience what it was like to grow up cherished and adored. Leah had asked him what that would feel like. Well, they could experience it together, couldn't they? They could create that experience and live it!

He just had to give in to it. Wholeheartedly. Be brave enough to accept that this was something he could do. That this was something he *wanted* to do.

So he understood Carol's fear. About losing something—someone—precious. And he was going to do his level best to not lose any of it now that it was within his reach.

CHAPTER ELEVEN

'THIRTY-TWO WEEKS. WHO'D have thought it?' Leah rubbed at her belly and glanced at Ben nervously. 'Never in my wildest dreams did I ever think I'd get to this point and now it's all so close! Two months more for me, and Sally due any day.' She bit her lip as she spoke her thoughts out loud. 'Do you think the placenta's moved?'

Ben placed his hand on her abdomen and felt his son kick in response. It was a good, strong kick, from a very strong baby. He was feeling very positive about the outcome, despite all the worries and concerns they'd had at the beginning.

'I hope so. But if it hasn't then we'll deal with it.'

'They'll want to admit me in case of sudden bleeding. But there's so much we haven't done yet. We haven't even touched the nursery, and Sally is due any time, and by the looks of things I'll have to put my baby down to sleep in a box! The cribs haven't been made up, nor the changing station, and we need to get in supplies—'

'Hey. It's okay. I'll sort it all out. If you have to be admitted I'll do the nursery.'

'But you have work—you'll be exhausted.'

'Stop worrying. It'll be fine.'

'Leah Hudson?' called a voice.

She gave him a *That's us* smile and lumbered to her

feet. But then she stopped and turned to face him, her face a mask of concern and fear.

'I'm scared. We've already dodged one bullet—what are the chances of me missing a second? The placenta will be over my cervix, and I'll bleed out, and something else will take my baby's life when all the time I've been worrying about the shape of my stupid uterus!'

Ben cupped her face and made her look at him before kissing her gently on the lips. 'It's okay to be scared, Leah, but we've *got* this, and you're in the best place you could ever be.'

She gripped his hands in hers. 'In hospital?'

He shook his head. 'No. With me.'

She smiled, bravely holding back the tears, and then she nodded before turning and making her way into the ultrasound room. She clambered up onto the bed, answering the sonographer's questions as she checked to make sure she had the right patient.

'And you're here today to check the position of the placenta?'

Leah nodded, lying down. 'Yes, the scan showed placenta praevia at twenty-weeks.'

'Okay...just some cold gel here and let's see what we shall see.' The sonographer smiled and began to move the probe over Leah's stomach.

Ben tensed as he watched the images, holding Leah's hand gently in his own. He knew how scared she was. How scared she'd been throughout the whole pregnancy. And he could understand why. She wanted this so much! To be a parent. To be a mum. And to have the chance to carry her own child, to give birth to a baby herself, was a privilege she'd never suspected she would get—and here she was, hoping that one last barrier would be overcome.

He hoped everything would be all right. His feelings

for this woman had grown exponentially over the last few months as his entire life had changed. He was heading towards a future he had never imagined for himself, and though that was terrifying he knew he could do it with Leah at his side.

She was perfect.

'It's moved!' The sonographer turned the screen so Leah could see. 'Look…it's no longer over the cervix.'

'Really?' Leah gazed at the screen in disbelief, tears trickling down her cheeks as she finally began to laugh with utter relief. 'Oh, my God! Ben, look at that!'

He laughed too. 'I see it! You're okay!'

'No hospital admission?'

The sonographer shook her head. 'No admission. Do you want a picture?'

Leah beamed a smile and squeezed his hand. 'Yes, we do.'

'Which one, do you think?' asked Leah.

Two days had passed since the scan and they stood in the room that would become their children's nursery, looking at the different patches of yellow paint that Leah had put on the walls. They had four different tester pots, ranging from a bright sunshine yellow right through to the palest hue, which seemed almost white.

'I don't know…' Ben answered.

'Well, what colour was your bedroom growing up?' she asked.

'It was blue.'

'Hah. Okay—the obvious choice.'

'What colour was *your* room?'

'White, mostly. Very clinical. And we weren't allowed to put up posters or anything.'

'Really?'

'Yeah. So I read books instead. Allowed myself to get lost in those worlds, where I could be anyone I wanted to be, wherever I wanted to be. Books gave me what I never had. So we'll need bookshelves in here, too.'

'Sounds lonely,' he said.

She nodded. 'Lonely sucks. I've been lonely. I've done it, seen it, got the T-shirt. Believe you me, you don't want to be there. Ooh!' She gripped her tummy.

'You okay?'

'Baby's kicking. *Hard.*'

He came over to her and pressed his hand against her rounded abdomen. She guided his hand to the right place…

A huge smile erupted on his face. 'I felt that!'

She laughed at his delight. 'A brand-new person, growing in my body. It's weird. Part of me doesn't want it to end.'

'Well, it will, at some point soon.'

'I know, but it was such a miracle in the first place!' She sighed, rubbing her belly, enjoying the feeling of her son moving inside her. 'And here we are choosing paint colours for the nursery.'

Ben nodded, looking at the walls, at the paint patches. 'That one,' he said, pointing at the paler yellow. 'I like that one.'

'Okay. Let's break out the pots!'

When the walls were painted, the nursery furniture moved in, the mural was on the wall and the mobiles were above the cribs, it suddenly hit Ben that this was going to be a room for his son. And Leah's other baby.

Real people, real babies, were going to grow up in *this* room.

They would learn to read in here, play with toys, develop their imaginations, forge their characters and come here as a place of retreat from the world. They would put posters on the walls and listen to music and bring friends here. They might slam the door after an argument, or be here whenever they were ill. This room would be a memory that would stay with their children *for ever*.

Leah was seven months pregnant now, and though he'd accepted the fact that he was going to be a father the fact that it was now so close was beginning to make him feel anxious.

Would he be a good father? Would he be able to impart wise words of wisdom? Would his son feel he could come and talk to him about anything?

He wanted to get this right—so much! And though Leah kept reassuring him that he'd already got loads of parenting experience under his belt, he still felt that he was a complete newbie.

It had been different in the past. This...this was completely new.

'We're ready!' Leah said, viewing the room from the doorway, a huge smile on her face.

She'd spent ages giving the nursery its finishing touches. The wardrobe was full of a selection of neutral-coloured baby clothes. Nappies were stacked in the corner. There were teddies and soft animals dotted all around, lots of cushions, and in the corner they'd put a rocking chair and footstool, for when Leah breastfed during the night. At least she *wanted* to try and breastfeed.

Next to the changing station were nappy sacks and a bin, cream for soothing sore skin and a stack of under-vests—because she'd read that babies often needed those changing at the same time, too.

Everything was perfect. Nothing was going to go wrong now. They were ready.

Leah had been reading book after book about to what to expect, and she'd come home with leaflets and ideas of what she wanted to try when it came to giving birth.

'We are *so* ready,' he said, then smiled and looked at her. Unsure whether they actually were.

They hadn't discussed his moving in. It seemed the logical thing to do, if they were going to raise a family together, but part of him really wanted to hold on to his flat, just in case it all went wrong. He couldn't tell her that, though, because then she'd want to know why he suspected that it would go wrong at all! But it was good to have a bolthole, right?

And Sally was due to give birth any day.

He felt anticipation about his own son arriving, but the thought of Leah's other baby getting here first made him anxious and uncomfortable.

What if he didn't connect with this other child? What if he treated it differently? He felt so distanced from it—almost as if it wasn't really happening. But this was *Leah's baby*. And he was with Leah. And he wanted to be the good guy and step up and be the father this baby girl should have. But he was already having trouble getting his head around having his *own* son and all that he would have to do to be a great father to *him*.

It all felt like too much. Troubling and disturbing whenever he thought about it. So he kept tossing those feelings to one side, thinking he would deal with them later, but knowing that time was a-ticking.

He'd never mentioned his concerns to Leah. He didn't want to frighten her—and that told him something. That his feelings for her were incredibly important and he didn't want to mess things up.

He told himself again that all new parents-to-be had doubts. It was natural, wasn't it?

And then the phone rang.

Leah answered the phone normally, but then her face changed and she gripped the receiver tightly.

'I'll be right there.'

She put the phone down and she was visibly shaking, so he guided her to a seat.

'What is it? Are you okay?'

'It's Sally. She's gone into labour.'

Right.

And then he felt it. As if something visible changed in the air. This was happening. Leah was going to have her other baby. The baby she had longed for—the *only* baby she'd thought she'd ever have. It was never going to be just the two of them any more.

She stood up. 'I have to go. I said I'd get there as soon as I could. I don't want to miss it!'

'Of course. Of course.'

He stood back and watched her get her things together. Her bag, her coat, her phone.

'Do you...er...need me to come with you?'

Part of him desperately wanted her to say, *Yes. Please come with me. You're part of this.* But he was also sensing something else that felt uncomfortable.

Leah wanted this baby. She was overwhelmed to be having her own child, too. But did she want *him* just as much? He'd never questioned her commitment to him until now. Until this point of change. This point of acceleration.

Everything would be different from now on. He wanted to feel needed. For being himself. For being a great person. Not just someone to help take care of her child. Not just someone who was taking on a father figure role only because she needed one.

He wanted to feel needed simply for being *him*. Because she couldn't live without him.

She'd never said anything. Neither of them had said anything. Not the three little words that the whole world wanted to hear.

His parents had never shown him that they wanted him. His father had said that he was an accident. An accident that had trapped him into a marriage of misery. He had never been in Leah's life equation. She'd always thought she would grow up and start her own family, be a single mother.

She wouldn't meet his gaze. 'You've got work, haven't you?'

'So do you, but you're going.'

She looked awkward. 'We can't both leave the department in the lurch. You go to work. I'll go and see Sally and I'll ring you when anything happens.'

'You're sure?'

It was a kick in the teeth. *Why* didn't she want him there for her child's birth? Did she feel he wasn't a part of this? Had he given her any vibes that had made her realise he hadn't yet got his head around the fact that she was having a baby that was nothing to do with him?

She smiled. 'Of course I'm sure. Look, I'd better be going. I'll talk to you later.'

'Be safe!' he called out as she closed the door behind her.

The flat seemed terribly empty without her in it. And when she came back it would be...

He tried to imagine her walking through the door holding a baby in her arms. Not *their* baby. *Her* baby.

I guess that means her maternity leave starts today.

She wouldn't be at work for a while now. She would be absorbed in the needs of her child. It would be different.

Had they ever really been just a twosome? Perhaps only on that one-night stand they'd had such a long time ago? That had been it. Those brief few hours before his sperm had reached her egg and then…fireworks. Blind-sided. Stunned. A baby. Then two babies. Then…

He didn't know what came next.

Ben gathered his things and set off for work. He knew what to expect there. Patients still had the capacity to surprise him, but it was a safe surprise. There were rules and procedures and protocols to follow. He was backed up by a team of specialists and the team had his back. It was why he liked working in A&E so much. The camaraderie there was different from other places, other wards. Life and death was very much on the line, but he could hold it at a distance. He didn't have to care. He could keep himself remote.

With Leah everything was up close and personal.

And now he had the capacity to be terribly hurt.

She could hear the baby crying already as she neared Sally's room. She was hit by a sudden sense of grief at having missed it—such a quick birth! She reverently knocked on the door and then opened it when someone called to say that she could come in.

There was a curtain over the entrance and she peeped around it and saw Sally, sitting up in bed, her arms holding a little baby against her chest, blankets wrapped around her to keep her warm.

Her gaze zoomed in on the baby, then moved up to her best friend's proud face. 'Sally?'

Her friend saw her and began to cry. 'Leah! Come and meet your daughter!'

Leah walked across the room and kissed Sally's cheek, then stooped down to look at her daughter's face. She looked as if she was asleep, her eyes closed, but every now and again she moved, or rubbed a tightly balled fist over her face and tried to gnaw at it, or she'd yawn and show a red gummy mouth.

Sally smiled. 'Your little girl.'

Yes! Her beautiful baby girl.

She had a name ready. 'Hey there, Phoebe. You're so beautiful. Can I hold her?'

'Of course you can.'

Sally passed her over and watched as Leah adjusted her hold to look down into her daughter's face. A little button nose, smooth, plump cheeks, a little tiny mouth that suddenly opened and yawned.

Leah beamed, settling into a chair at the side of Sally's bed. 'Oh, look at you! You're gorgeous!' She looked up at her friend. 'That was so quick! You only phoned me about forty minutes ago!'

Sally nodded. 'I tried to hold on for you, but...when a baby wants to come, it comes!'

'And your last delivery was quick, wasn't it?'

'Just two hours with Jack.'

Leah nodded. She remembered. 'I can't believe I missed it!'

'Well, you won't miss the next one. You'll be the star of the show.'

The baby kicked in Leah's belly, as if to agree. But Leah couldn't stop staring down at her daughter. Baby Phoebe was beautiful.

'Isn't she perfect?'

'She is. The midwife checked her over and everything's fine. All ten fingers and ten tiny toes.'

Leah looked up. 'And you're okay?'

Sally nodded. 'I am.'

'No regrets?'

'How could there be? Seeing her there in your arms, where she was always meant to be.'

'I can't thank you enough. I really can't.'

'You don't have to.'

'Hello, baby. Hello, Phoebe. Oh, my goodness, I love you so much already…'

She couldn't quite believe she was holding her own daughter in her hands. She looked so little!

'How heavy is she?'

'Six pounds exactly,' said Sally.

Leah beamed a smile at her friend. 'And you? how are *you* doing? You know I will always, *always* be in your debt.'

'I'm fine—and don't be silly. You don't owe me anything. I'd do it all over again if I had to.' She raised an eyebrow. 'Not that you'll take me up on that, seeing as you seem to be able to do it yourself now.' She laughed.

Leah smiled. She inhaled the scent of her daughter's head. 'She smells perfect—and look at her hair!'

'Same colour as yours.'

'I hope she looks like me as she grows up—though I guess there'll always be parts of her which will belong to her father, whoever he is.'

Sally lay her head back on the pillows. 'Just think of him as a good man who did a good thing. And now you have Ben, too. You're very lucky.'

Leah smiled. 'I am, aren't I?' And she kissed the top of Phoebe's head and nestled down in the chair for the best snuggle ever.

When Ben got to the cubicle of his next patient he found him fast asleep on the bed, bedraggled and smelling like a brewery.

'Mr Anderson?' He gave his patient's shoulder a little

shake and slowly the man woke up, blinking his eyes at the light.

'Wow… S'bright in here.'

'Mr Anderson, it says here that you had a fall and bumped your head. Can you tell me how that happened?'

Though Ben had a suspicion, he didn't want to leap to any conclusions just because the man was drunk. He might have an underlying condition that had caused him to fall.

Mr Anderson pulled himself up into a sitting position. 'I don't know. One moment I'm walking along, minding my own business, the next minute I'm on the ground.'

'I see. Were you dizzy at all before you fell?'

'No. Can I have a drink of water?'

'I need to examine you first. Have you fallen before?'

'I fell in love with a woman once!' He laughed at his own small joke. But then his face darkened and he looked as if he was on the verge of tears. 'But she left me. Broke my heart, she did. Said I was a failure as a man.' He looked up at Ben and pointed his finger. 'Don't risk it! It's not worth it! Look what she's done to me! Are you married?'

Ben smiled. 'No.'

'Best way, my friend. Stay single. Women do nothing but break your heart. Look at mine.'

He pulled apart his shirt to reveal his hairy chest, and Ben couldn't help but notice the rather painful-looking rash there.

'That looks like shingles, Mr Anderson. Have you been feeling under the weather recently?'

His patient shrugged and slumped back down on the bed, clearly eager to get some more sleep.

'Mr Anderson? I need you to stay awake so that I

can fully examine you. How much alcohol have you drunk tonight?'

'Just the one…' His eyes blinked open again.

'The one what? Beer?'

His patient laughed. 'One litre!'

Ben smiled. He was used to dealing with drunks. Not only in his professional life, but also in his personal one. It brought back many memories of what it had been like trying to talk to his parents, trying to get their attention. Trying to get them to concentrate, just for once! But he didn't get angry any more, as he had when he was a young teenager. Now he saw it for what it was.

A hiding place.

His mother and father had been hiding from the consequences of becoming parents when they hadn't been ready. Hiding from the stresses and strains of real life because normal life was too hard, too painful, too difficult. It numbed them and kept them safe from hurt.

Mostly, anyway.

What was Mr Anderson hiding from? Obviously there was heartache in his past. He'd already alluded to that. But didn't everyone have heartache in their past?

Ben did. Leah did. His parents, his patients, his siblings. But not everyone turned to booze to get away from it. What made someone strong and another weak? Or did strength and weakness not have anything to do with it at all? Perhaps it was down to whether you had an addictive personality?

Life was tough for everyone. Should people be punished for how they chose to deal with it?

If it hurts others, maybe they should?

Ben found a small wound on the back of Mr Anderson's head. He closed it with some scalp glue and wrote a prescription for some Acyclovir that would treat his shingles. Then he allowed the man to stay on the bed and sleep off the worst of the alcohol, giving instructions for him to be checked on regularly.

As he wrote his notes at the doctors' desk his thoughts went to Leah. He hadn't heard from her yet. Was she coaching Sally through every contraction? Was she getting more and more nervous? Was she feeling stressed?

He hoped she was enjoying every second of it. Watching her future changing right before her eyes.

Was there going to be a baby in her home tonight?

His heart pounded in his chest as he thought about it. Time to step up to the plate, no matter his fears. Time to be the man he knew he had to be.

Time to stop running.

Leah felt thrilled to give Phoebe her first bottle. Sally had provided some colostrum—the first form of milk that was so important—and expressed it into a bottle so Leah could feed her. She sat beside Sally's bed as she did so.

Phoebe mouthed the teat a little and then began to suck, making cute little swallowing sounds of satisfaction.

Tears came unbidden to Leah's eyes. This was amazing! To hold her *own* baby! Phoebe had her hair, her eyes and a tiny button nose. She was a miniature version of herself.

As she looked down at her daughter's face she tried to find features that might be from her unknown father— the anonymous sperm donor. She couldn't find any. But they had to be there. Somewhere.

Perhaps when she's a little older I'll spot them?

'So, how's it going between you and Ben?' asked Sally, relaxing back against her mountain of pillows.

Leah looked up at her and smiled. 'It's going great.'

'Has he moved in yet?'

She looked back at her daughter. 'We haven't discussed it.'

She wasn't sure if she was even *ready* to discuss it. What if he said no? It was a big ask. Was it better not to tempt fate? She wanted to continue to enjoy what she had with Ben and everything was going brilliantly right now. What if he moved in and it didn't work out? That would break her heart.

'It's a big step,' said Sally.

She nodded. 'It is.'

'He'd be lucky to have you, you know.'

She smiled. 'Thanks.'

'I mean it. You're special, Leah. You have such a big heart, considering what you've been through.'

'*You* have the big heart. Doing this for me. I can't imagine how you must feel, going through labour and then giving the baby away. Going home with empty arms.'

She could feel the tears burning in her eyes again. How other women managed to do it, she had no idea. It took immense amounts of bravery and courage.

'She was never mine.' Sally said. 'That makes it easier.'

'I love you so much, Sal. I can never thank you enough.'

Phoebe had finished her small amount of expressed milk and had dropped off the bottle into a deep sleep.

'Should I wake her to burp her?' Leah asked.

'Probably.'

Leah stood up and lifted Phoebe against her shoulder, began patting her on the back. She saw Sally's eyes drop to her own swollen stomach.

'Not much longer till you're the one in this bed. Nervous?'

'Of course! But I also can't wait.'

Phoebe let out a small burp and Sally smiled.

'You're going to be an amazing mum.'

He'd been trying to call her all day, but the department had been rushed off its feet. There'd been a major incident late on in the day—a fire in a block of flats—and there'd been a few burn victims, as well as those who needed treatment for smoke inhalation. He'd barely had time to breathe, and when he had finally been free to go home he'd worked two hours past the end of his shift.

At his locker, he picked up his mobile phone and tried to call Leah, but it went straight to voicemail.

'Hey, it's me. Just thought I'd check in and see how Sally's getting on. Let me know when you can. I'm going home now, to take a shower, so I might not hear the phone ring if you call me, but I should be at yours about eight o'clock tonight. Let me know if you need me to come over to the hospital and wait with you, or whatever you and Sally might need. Speak to you soon—bye.'

He stared at his phone and checked his messages one last time, but there was nothing there. He'd felt sure there would be *something* from Leah by the time he got to his locker, but there was nothing. He hoped nothing was wrong. That Sally's labour was going okay. But he couldn't ring to check because he didn't even know which hospital Sally had gone to.

Why hadn't he asked such a simple question?

Because I still feel—somehow—like it isn't any of my business.

His forehead touched the locker door. What the hell was he doing? Getting all confused—that was what! He'd tried so hard to hide his doubts and his fears about all this. Telling himself he was happy to be a father. And he was! It had taken a moment or two to get used to the idea but he *was* happy. Happy to step up and father Leah's surrogate baby, too.

But had some of his old fears been quietly stewing in the background so he'd never asked too many questions about Sally? He'd not wanted to upset anyone. He'd not wanted to pry too much or force his own needs on Leah, worried about how she might react.

Was this love?

He didn't know. He'd deliberately stopped himself from falling in love with anyone his entire life, so he had nothing to equate it to—but it hurt, damn it, and he was pretty sure he was caught up in its web.

He was just about to head for home when his mobile rang in his jacket pocket. He fumbled for it in haste, and was instantly delighted to see Leah's name flash up on screen.

'Hi, how's it going?'

'She's here, Ben! Phoebe. And she's perfect. Ten tiny fingers and ten tiny toes.'

He felt a wave of relief and sat down on one of the benches in the locker room. 'That's brilliant. Congratulations!'

'She looks like me. I've fed her and changed her, and the nurse is going to show me how to give her a bath later.'

'Fantastic. Do you want me to come over? I could bring you both home. I bet you don't have the car seat with you.'

'Oh, don't worry about that. They're not sending Sally or Phoebe home until tomorrow morning, so why don't you go home and get some rest?'

'Me? I'm fine.' He was lying. But he wasn't going to tell her he was exhausted—not when he felt it was important to be there for Leah and this new baby.

We have a daughter now. Phoebe.

He loved the name.

'You should rest up. Get one last night of unbroken sleep,' said Leah.

'What about you?'

'I'm staying here with Sally.'

'Is she okay?'

'Sally? She's doing well. Amazing, in fact.'

'So when do you want me to come and pick you up in the morning? I'm on late shift at the hospital, so I could come over at about ten?'

'I'll call you and let you know.'

Something wasn't right. But what?

Still afraid to pry, he simply said, 'Okay. I'll speak to you tomorrow, then?'

'Sure. I can't wait for you to see her, Ben! She's so beautiful.'

'Just like her mother. Congratulations again.'

'Thank you.'

Despite his exhaustion, he decided to go to Leah's flat. He knew where she kept the spare key in case of emergencies. He would stop off at the supermarket on his way and get lots of healthy food to fill the fridge. Then he would clean and vacuum, so that when she got home with the baby she wouldn't have to worry about anything else except baby care. It would be a nice surprise for her.

He went to his home and showered first, then grabbed a quick sandwich and headed out to the shop. He picked up fruit and vegetables, soup and rice and pasta—lots of things that were healthy and quick to cook. Then he headed down the baby aisle and happily looked at all the products, trying to think if they'd missed anything.

With his car full of shopping bags he drove to Leah's

place, parked up, grabbed the bags and began to walk up the front path.

And then frowned.

The lights were on.

Had they left them on the last time they were there? He couldn't remember. Usually Leah was very good at stuff like that.

He put down the bags on the doorstep and fumbled under the pretend rock that was really a key safe. He pulled out the spare key and inserted it into the lock.

And when he opened the door he could hear a baby crying.

His heart began to pound. Why was there a baby crying?

He rushed through the flat, finding the source of the sound in the nursery.

Leah stood there, baby Phoebe over her shoulder, patting her on the back, trying to get her to stop crying. Leah saw him and her eyes widened. Then she smiled at him. A smile that said, *Please don't be angry with me.*

'You're home,' he said, frowning.

Phoebe sure had a good set of lungs on her. He tried to look at the baby. Tried to see if she looked like her mother. But he couldn't tell from this angle.

'Yes.'

'But you said you weren't coming home until tomorrow morning?'

'I know. I'm sorry, I just… Look, can I get her settled first and then we can talk? I don't want the first thing she hears in the flat to be arguing.'

'Sure.' He left the nursery and headed to the kitchen. For some reason he felt furious! Furious that he'd been lied to. Furious that he'd been kept out of the loop.

Why hadn't she wanted him to know she was at home?

He slammed a kitchen cupboard closed in his anger as he searched for the teabags, and then he slowed down and took a deep breath. He would not let her confusing treatment of him make him into an angry monster. That was not what Phoebe needed to hear. He knew what it felt like to grow up listening to parents who couldn't talk to one another without shouting the odds.

Leah would have a reason. A good one. He just didn't know what it was yet.

Ben stood in the kitchen for a long time, listening to Phoebe cry, and then slowly the crying became whimpering, then sniffling and then quiet.

By the time Leah made it out of the nursery and came into the kitchen where he stood his mug was empty.

He didn't want to meet her eyes. Didn't want to see any rejection of him in her face. But he couldn't help himself, and when he did look at her he realised she'd been crying too.

His anger disappeared in an instant. He needed to comfort her and make her feel better. 'You okay?'

She sniffed and wiped away her tears using the sleeve that she'd pulled over her hand. 'Yeah. That was tougher than I ever thought it would be. She wouldn't stop crying. She just wouldn't! Ever since I took her from the hospital. Do you think she knows I'm not the one who carried her?'

'Of course not.'

'Then why did she cry so much? Nothing I did could settle her.'

'She's settled now.'

'Thank goodness.'

He turned and switched on the kettle to make her a fresh drink, and when it was done, and he'd passed it over, he followed her into the lounge and sat opposite her on the couch. He watched her sip at her drink, her face tired. He wanted to ask her something. Something important, but he was afraid of the answer.

'Why didn't you tell me you were already home?'

She looked down and away. 'I don't know.'

'Yes, you do. Tell me why.'

She shook her head and let out a big breath in resignation. She had to tell him the truth.

'I just…just wanted to spend some alone time with her. Just me and Phoebe. Before I let the rest of the world in.' She looked at him, imploring him with her eyes. 'Please understand. When I set out to do this originally I thought I'd be on my own, and I was so looking forward to the moment when I first brought her home and it would just be me and her, looking at each other, learning about each other, getting to know one another.'

'But your life's not like that now. You're not on your own. I'm with you. Or at least I *think* I'm with you. It felt like you were shutting me out, when I found out you were home. Do you know how that made me feel?'

She shook her head. 'I'm sorry. I didn't think about that.'

'I felt excluded. Like I'm not a part of this. You want me to be Phoebe's father, and I'm happy to be—you know that…despite everything—but you went to the hospital alone and brought her home alone and kept it from me.' He looked deeply into her eyes. 'Do you want me here, or not?'

'I do! It's just…'

'What?'

'I've never had to rely on anyone else. Never had to *answer* to anyone else. I'm new to this and I'm feeling my way.'

'You're a mother now. And if we're to build this family and build it right—the way we both want, so we can have the secure family unit we dream of—then you have to let me in!'

'Sometimes you hold yourself back, Ben. You say you want this, and that you want to be with me, but you keep a part of yourself held back all the time. It's like… I don't know…like you're trying to protect yourself from getting hurt. I can feel it even if you don't say it.'

He stared at her. Had he been holding himself back?

'I need someone who's into this one hundred percent,' she said.

'Then you have to let me in. You have to *let* me be part of this. How am I supposed be into it one hundred percent, to get to know Phoebe, if you don't even tell me she's home?'

At that moment Phoebe woke again. They could hear her crying in the nursery.

'Okay. I'm sorry. I acted without thinking of your feelings and that was wrong.'

He nodded and stepped past her, heading to the nursery, towards the crying. And though his stomach was in knots, and he wasn't sure that what he was doing was right, he stepped over to the crib and scooped up Phoebe into his arms. Her little face was red from crying, and all scrunched up, but he could see she was a pretty little thing—and so darn cute in her pale pink baby onesie.

He hugged her in close and began to bob and sway gently, humming a tune he'd used to hum to his younger brother and sister.

It felt surprisingly good to hold a baby in his arms again.

His baby.

Whether he was the biological father or not didn't matter. He was this baby's dad.

Soon enough Phoebe's tears stopped as she listened, and she seemed really happy to be in his secure embrace.

He beamed a smile at her, pleased as punch that he hadn't forgotten how to do this, that he still had a way with babies, and when he turned around he saw Leah in the nursery doorway.

She looked jealous. 'You have a magic touch.'

'Nonsense. You just have to know what you're doing.'

He said it without thinking, and when he looked up again to say something about how Phoebe looked like her mother Leah had gone from the doorway. He could hear her doing things in the kitchen—moving about, emptying the dishwasher.

Looking down at Phoebe, he found it hard right there and then to remember why he had fought this for so long. It was so different once they were in your arms, and they were so little, and needed your help and protection. He'd forgotten how much he missed this stage. How much he'd enjoyed it. The anger was gone now that he could hold her.

'Hello, Phoebe. I'm your daddy.'

Leah had only been asleep for about an hour when Phoebe's crying woke her. 'I'll go and do the bottle.'

Ben rubbed at his face. 'She might not want food.'

But she was already out of bed, pulling on her robe. 'It's just over two hours since her last feed. I bet you she's hungry.'

The midwives had said to her before she'd left the hospital that eventually she would begin to learn her baby's different cries. Hunger cries, *I-need-my-nappy-changed* cries, *I-need-you-to-burp-me* cries. But so far Leah thought they all sounded the same. Indignant and angry and upset. If Phoebe had been in her teenage years

Leah was sure she'd be giving her sullen stares, or slamming her bedroom door, or stomping away screaming that she never wanted to speak to Leah ever again.

She smiled at the thought. *I'm already thinking of her being a teenager!* Which was really quite funny, considering that she'd thought she'd never get to be a mother, because of her uterus, and never thought of trusting someone to carry a baby for her.

And then she'd met Sally. Her best friend whom she'd known for years. She loved Sally inside and out, but there'd still been some jealousy when Sally had become pregnant so easily and carried Phoebe. Especially at the beginning, before Leah had met Ben.

Why did it happen so easily for some women?

Sally was a natural mother. It came so easily for her. Leah could only hope that she was half the woman Sally was—then she would be a good mum. It was a thought that had kept her awake for most of the night already, because all Phoebe had done so far since Leah had brought her home was cry in her arms.

Did Phoebe miss Sally's heartbeat? Her scent?

Her insecurities were going crazy. Her daughter seemed to be resisting her, and she couldn't work out where she was going wrong?

This time was meant to be magical. So why wasn't it?

Was it because Sally had been cuddling Phoebe skin to skin before Leah had got to the hospital? They'd had that time to bond, for the baby to imprint on Sally so she hadn't imprinted on *her.*

Maybe I'm just being silly. Paranoid. A typical new mother.

She waddled slowly into the nursery, wincing at the intense crying that filled her ears, and scooped up her daughter, hushing her and cooing and trying her best to get her to settle. But all Phoebe wanted to do was cry, big tears trickling down her plump little cheeks. Her whole body seemed tense, angry and upset.

Leah felt like crying herself. She wished she could bawl her head off, too, but her sense of responsibility told her that she couldn't do that. She needed to keep it together.

She went into the kitchen to get the bottle ready, but Ben was already there.

'Do you want me to take her?' Ben asked.

'No!' she answered, more sternly than she'd thought she would. She changed her tone to a more conciliatory one. 'I have to learn to settle her myself.'

'Okay.' Ben dribbled some of the milk onto his wrist to test its temperature. 'It seems fine.'

'Well? Is it or isn't it?'

He looked at her, confused. 'It's fine.'

'Good.' She took the bottle from him and gave it to Phoebe, who began to suck hungrily. Now that the noise had stopped, and she was feeling a trifle triumphant, she waddled back to the nursery, so she could sit in the rocker whilst Phoebe fed.

Ben followed her. 'Do you want me to stay up with you or…?'

'You've got work tomorrow. You go to sleep. Me and Phoebe need this time together.'

'You're sure?'

'I'm sure.' She gave him a quick smile, remembering what he'd said earlier about being left out, then continued to look down at her daughter.

Ben disappeared from the doorway and she felt herself exhale a long, low breath. Why did she feel so tense? Why did she feel that his presence made her antsy and short-fused? Was it just pregnancy hormones? She was big now, swollen and heavy, and each day she was exhausted by teatime. Perhaps it wasn't Ben at all?

As Phoebe drank, contented little murmurings emitting from her throat, she took a moment to stare at her little girl. She had very fair eyebrows, almost invisible, but lovely thick, long eyelashes. She was perfect. Beautiful and perfect.

And mine. I have a daughter now.

That thought made her so happy! She'd never had a true family before. None that she knew of, anyway. Technically, they must be out there. She might have treated her mother or her father or any relative in A&E and she wouldn't have known it.

But Phoebe was hers. Her own flesh and blood after thirty odd years of being alone in the world. This was where it all began—with this little baby in her arms. They would love each other and grow together, making their own little customs and having their own little traditions. Maybe she would buy Phoebe a special bracelet? It could become an heirloom that Phoebe would pass down through her own children. So that no one in their family would ever feel that they didn't have roots or a history that they could look back on.

That would be nice. That sense of belonging. Because they belonged to each other now, and when her son came they would be an even bigger family and Phoebe would be a sister. A big sister. And she would have a ripe tale to tell her schoolfriends as to why she and her brother had only two months between them. They would even be in the same school year!

As Phoebe finished her milk Leah pulled the bottle away and for a brief moment all was fine. Phoebe seemed content, happy to try and nuzzle her tightly screwed up fists.

And in that moment Leah looked into her daughter's eyes and thought, *I can do this. It's going to be okay. We're going to be all right.*

And then the crying began again.

Leah resignedly put Phoebe over her shoulder and started trying to burp her. This was an incredible, amazing day and she was *not* going to let the crying upset her.

CHAPTER TWELVE

BEN HAD NOT wanted to leave them both to go to work. Leah had looked frazzled and exhausted when he'd left that morning, her face pale, her hair all over the place, dark circles beneath her eyes.

She'd spent all night trying to get Phoebe to settle, and though he'd got up many times and asked to take the baby she had shot him down—more than once.

'No, Ben, I need to do this myself.'

'We need to do it together. You can feed her. I'll settle her. Teamwork—see?'

'She has to let *me* settle her. She has to learn.'

And no matter how much he'd argued that she needed to rest, that Phoebe could probably sense Leah's distress, she'd refused to let him help and had kept sending him back to bed, so he could sleep.

But he hadn't slept. He'd heard Phoebe crying all night, off and on, and he'd kept picturing in his mind Leah pacing the room, or rocking back and forth in the rocking chair, trying her hardest, hoping and praying that Phoebe would settle.

She definitely had a good set of lungs on her—that was for sure! He wanted to step in. To help. But Leah was being quite clear that she didn't want that.

He could understand why Leah was so determined to

do it herself, but they were a couple. They were in this together and she needed to let him help her. She wasn't going to get a medal for perseverance. They had to find what worked, and if he was available to help then she should take advantage of that so that she could rest. She needed rest. She was seven months pregnant with their son.

At work, he grabbed his first patient file, determined to work long and hard so that the hours of the day passed quickly. The triage chart revealed that his patient was a quadriplegic with a feeding tube issue.

'Phillip Underwood?'

A young boy in a motorised wheelchair began to drive himself forward. Behind him trailed a woman, carrying bags and coats and all manner of other paraphernalia. He smiled at her and led the way to a cubicle.

'Hi there. I'm Mr Willoughby. It says here that you have a problem with your feeding tube?'

Phillip nodded and lifted up his top. His arms were skeletal, with barely any muscle mass. 'My feeding tube has come out from my stomach.'

Ben looked and saw that the only thing wrong was that the external bumper had slid down the tube and was not in place against the gauze next to the skin. 'This?'

'Yes.'

He put on some gloves and slid the bumper back into position so that it nestled against the gauze. 'All done!'

'That's it? That's all I had to do?' asked Philip.

'Yep!' Ben smiled, glad to have seen that this was an easy fix.

'Well, *that's* kind of embarrassing. And annoying. Why didn't anyone tell me I could do that?'

'They probably missed it out. There's so much to tell you when you first get a feeding tube.'

'But I had to come all this way and sit in your waiting room for hours. I could have stayed at home!'

Ben could understand his frustration, but wondered if perhaps he had been told how to do it, but he hadn't been able to take it all in?

Phillip's mother smiled. 'Thank you, Doctor. Phil insisted on coming. He's so determined to be independent and he wouldn't let anyone else touch it. We're sorry to have wasted your time.'

'Not at all. Glad to have helped.'

'So we can go?'

'You can go.' He held open the curtain to the cubicle and watched Phillip drive himself out.

His mother smiled at him as she passed, looking for all the world like a pack mule. 'I don't know where he gets his stubbornness from, but ever since the accident he's been determined to do everything by himself. He gets really mad if people try to help.'

Ben nodded and smiled as she left, knowing exactly how frustrated Phillip's mother felt. But it had felt good to come here and help *someone*.

All he wanted to do was help. Why was that so bad? Why was it seen as a terrible thing? It wasn't as if Leah was accepting charity from Ben. They were a couple. They were supposed to do things together.

Phillip was a young boy. A teenager. He was supposed to be headstrong and determined. But if he wasn't careful he'd take on too much and become overwhelmed. He'd had a life-changing accident, He had a PEG-tube. Quadriplegia. He had to accept his new limits. Had to accept that at the beginning he might need an extra hand. At least until he became familiar with his new situation.

There was nothing wrong in accepting help.

Perhaps I ought to be more insistent when I offer help to Leah?

He didn't want to offend her, and he knew she wanted to be a great mother more than anything, but she wasn't alone any more. She wasn't a single mother and she didn't have to power through.

How could he show her that he was determined to be a father and to be involved if she wouldn't let him help? Did she doubt him? Because Phoebe wasn't his?

That didn't matter to him!

They could share this experience.

If only she'd let him…

Leah woke with a start, blinking furiously as she realised she'd fallen asleep on the couch. Beside her, still sleeping, was Phoebe, wrapped in a blanket. Scared, she sat up and scooped her daughter into her arms.

She could have fallen off the couch! I can't fall asleep like that again!

Disturbed by Leah moving her, Phoebe began to snuffle and let out cries of protest at being woken too soon.

She had a wet nappy, so Leah stood up to change it.

It was only when she was in the nursery that she realised how totally unpractical it was to have the changing station where it was. Yes, it allowed her to change Phoebe's nappy in a standing position, so she wasn't bent over, but she had to let go of Phoebe to pick up the nappies, which were stacked on the floor further away. She'd managed before only because Ben had been there, helping her.

Why was she finding that situation difficult? She'd been so worried about Phoebe's arrival, fretting that Ben wouldn't take to her because she wasn't his child, even though he'd insisted he would be there for her and both children.

I thought I was so lucky! To have a man like Ben, willing to step up and do that. And yet now that she's here...

She felt something inside. Something huge and immovable. An insistence and a determination within herself that *she* needed to do this. To show that she could be a mother. Not just a normal mother, but a *great* mother. And yet so far she'd missed her daughter's birth and hadn't been able to stop her from crying.

She felt as if Phoebe knew she wasn't the woman who had carried her. As if Phoebe was somehow protesting that she wanted to go back to Sally's arms. Hear Sally's heartbeat once again.

The fear of failing was growing bigger each hour. Leah knew it was ridiculous, but she couldn't get it out of her head, and so she was determined to prove to herself—and her daughter—that she could do this. That she could make Phoebe happy.

And that was why it was so hard to let Ben in. The one time Ben had held Phoebe she had quietened and gone to sleep straight away, as if he had some magical touch—and he wasn't related to her at all!

Well, this is just ridiculous, I have to learn to do this on my own!

She changed Phoebe and put her in the crib whilst she rearranged the nappy changing station, bringing all the supplies to within arm's reach. Then she scooped up Phoebe and decided to take her for a walk in her pushchair. They both needed some fresh air—it would do them good—and if they were only out for about twenty minutes she'd be back in time for Phoebe's next feed.

I'll just walk around the block.

But she'd never got a baby ready to go out before. Or

tried to put the pushchair up on her own. And though she'd watched the demonstration in the shop, and it had looked easy, now she was on her own it wasn't. By the time she finally got it up, and had fetched Phoebe's coat and some blankets, time was up and Phoebe was ready for her feed.

The crying began again, in earnest.

Are babies meant to cry this much?

She prepped the feed, shaking the bottle to mix the formula and then warming it up, but by the time she was ready to try and feed her daughter Phoebe was almost apoplectic with rage. She was so hungry and so upset that no matter how much Leah tried to get the teat into her mouth Phoebe didn't even notice.

'Come on! Come on, Phoebe, *please*!' All it would take was for her daughter to calm down enough to notice the teat. Then she would be happy.

Determined to settle her daughter, Leah pressed on, trying to remain calm herself despite the onset of tears.

She didn't know what to do and so, terrified that the neighbours might start complaining about child cruelty or something crazy, she put her screaming baby into the car seat and began to drive.

Maybe she was doing something wrong? But how many ways could you get a baby to drink milk? Surely it wasn't meant to be this hard? Well, seeing as Ben seemed to have the magical touch with Phoebe *he* would have to sort this out!

She hates me.

She got to the hospital and parked in the dropping off bay, then scooped up Phoebe and the bottle and took her crying child into A&E.

The people in the waiting room looked at her with

suspicion and irritation as she walked straight past them and into the bowels of the hospital.

Phoebe's face was bright red and wet with streaming tears, and just when Leah thought that she might end up the same way she saw Ben, who emerged from a cubicle, frowning.

'Leah? Is something wrong?'

'Ben!'

It was the kindness in his voice, the concerned look on his face at seeing her, that tipped her over the edge. She burst into tears and hiccupped her way through an explanation, and before she knew it he'd scooped the baby from her arms and was rocking her and hushing her and, yes—typical—had got the bottle into Phoebe's mouth. She was finally feeding. Sniffing and gulping as tears silently slid down her plump cheeks.

Leah stared at him with a jealousy she didn't want to feel, but she couldn't help it. Why was it so easy for him when it was so difficult for her? When it had been her dream to be a mother?

'There you go, Pheebs. There's a good girl,' he cooed, watching her with a smile as she fed.

Her temper was settling, and she paused from her feed to breathe every now and again while she calmed down as the milk hit her stomach.

Ben looked over at Leah, tucked the bottle in position with his chin and stroked her arm. 'You okay?'

She shook her head. 'I can't seem to settle her or feed her. She screams non-stop. The only person she seems to like is you.'

'That's nonsense.'

'It's true! Look at her! Look how fine she is with you! But I can't keep bringing her here for feeds. I can't live with her in this hospital just so you can take over and show me what a crap mother I am!'

She sniffed and wiped her face with her sleeve, unable to believe that she was in such a predicament. This was not how it was meant to be. This was not how she'd imagined motherhood to be.

He'd tried to tell her, hadn't he? Once before. That families could be hard. Maybe he was right, and she should have listened more to his dire warnings, because quite clearly she was in some terrible reality she couldn't escape.

In her head she'd pictured a dreamy vision of contentment. Just like the mothers she saw in magazines or in films. Surrounded by a rosy glow as they rocked their peaceful, quiet, happy babies to sleep. She had intended to be the best mother in the world! And she was failing at it. Already.

The thought angered her.

'What is it?' Ben asked.

'Nothing. I... Let me take her now she's settled. You're working. I shouldn't have come here like this.'

'It's okay. I was due a break anyway.'

'Ben, give me Phoebe.'

He looked up at her firm, *don't-mess-with-me* tone and passed her over. He looked reluctant, and she almost laughed at the ridiculousness of this situation. Ben hadn't even wanted kids! And yet he was a natural!

She felt terrible for feeling jealous, so she sucked in a deep breath and decided that, no matter what, she had to be strong. Rise to the challenge. She was brand-new at this. As was Phoebe. They just hadn't had time to get to know one another yet. They were both learning.

And soon she'd have another baby to look after, too.

'I'm sorry, I'd better go.'

'Stay. Just for a little longer. Till she's finished her feed and she's burped and changed. Then she'll sleep in the car on the way home.'

She knew he was trying to be sensible, but all she heard was the implication that she wouldn't be able to handle Phoebe after the feed, getting her winded and settled. Even *he* doubted her abilities to be a mother. She just *knew* he had to be doubting his decision to get involved with her if she was going to be this bad a carer for their child.

She felt rage fill her. Hurt encompassing her.

'Thanks. But I need to learn how to do this. I'd better go.'

Confused, he bent to kiss her cheek, but she moved away instead, to pick up the baby bag, knowing that if he kissed her, if he showed her kindness, she would cry again. She would get Phoebe safely into her car seat and hopefully she would settle on the short drive home.

She'd had a wobble—that was all. Every new mother was entitled to have one of those, wasn't she? A little panic?

But as she pushed Phoebe back through the hospital and out into the car park the thoughts descended like vultures.

What if Phoebe *didn't* settle?

What then?

'Leah!' Ben called out after her, but she walked purposefully away, leaving him wondering if he'd somehow said something to upset her.

He'd been trying to help. Seeing her struggle like she was, was breaking his heart.

He knew how much she wanted this—to be a mother. And not just to be a mother, but to be a *great* mother. The best there ever was!

By doing so, she hoped to blot out the past. To show that what her own mother had done to her would end there and that she, Leah, would show the love, the compassion, the patience, the adoration for her own baby that she'd never experienced herself.

She never spoke about it much, but he knew how much of a dent in her confidence her childhood had been. Abandoned? Dumped like trash? The implication was there, wasn't it? She'd been put in a bin, after all.

He admired her strength and fortitude, and the fact that she was usually such an optimist, but something had changed since Phoebe's arrival. It wasn't going the way Leah had hoped it would and he could see she was struggling—especially being so close to giving birth herself. She was bravely trying to act as if she wasn't, and that was why he was so keen to step in when he could and help out.

He loved her. He could admit that to himself now. And seeing her hurting like this broke his heart. He wanted to be there for her.

Perhaps being at work right now wasn't the best thing? Perhaps he needed to take a day or two off? Just to help her out. He intended to take full paternity leave when their son was born, but they had Phoebe *now* and Leah needed help.

Walking to the doctors' desk, he picked up the phone and called through to Tom Riley, head of the department. The phone rang a few times, and then it was picked up.

'Tom? It's Ben Willoughby.'

'Hi, Ben, what's up?'

'Look, I know we're swamped, and we're already a doctor down with Leah not being here, but any chance I could take the day off? And maybe tomorrow?'

There was a pause. 'Are you not well?'

'No, I'm fine. It's Leah. She's not coping with the baby and I'm worried about her. She's just been here in tears. She's struggling, Tom. Hard. She needs my support.'

'Well, I appreciate you being honest with me and not spinning me a story. Can you give me an hour or two? I'll see if I can arrange someone to swap shifts with you.'

He let out a sigh of relief. Tom was a good guy. 'Yeah. Sure. Thanks, Tom, I appreciate it.'

'No problem, mate. I'll give you a call when I've got news.'

'Cheers.' He put down the phone and worried at a small bit of skin next to his fingernail.

Was he doing the right thing?

The image of Leah's crying, sobbing face told him that he was.

He sat down and began to input his latest set of patient notes.

Phoebe had slept in the car on the way home. For a blissful half hour or so Leah had been able to convince herself that she'd cracked it and that she'd be able to do this. But when she'd had to remove the car seat from the car and carry Phoebe inside she had begun to snuffle and wake up.

'No, no...please don't wake up. Please keep sleeping. *Please!*' she whispered, closing the door shut behind her softly and carrying the car seat into the living room, setting it on the floor, rocking it gently.

But Phoebe was waking up and she was not happy.

Sighing heavily, Leah sank onto the couch opposite her and put her head in her hands, exhausted and at the end of her tether. She also began to cry, sobbing in great gulps of air as she cried and cried, mourning the fact that she wasn't an Earth mother. A natural.

Inside her, her son began to kick hard—as if he, too, was deciding to act out.

She knew she ought to get Phoebe out of the car seat and try to comfort her, though she didn't really want to. She knew she had to try. Ben the baby whisperer wasn't here. Someone had to do it! She had to step up! To stop being so pathetic and giving in.

She knelt forward and undid the clasp of the car seat. She scooped Phoebe up, lying her on her lap and removing her coat. Underneath, she found that Phoebe had dirtied her nappy, so she took her through to the nursery to clean her and change her, all the time feeling detached from reality as she went through the motions.

There was no point in saying *There, there* or *Shh...* or singing nursery rhymes, because nothing worked with this child. Nothing *she* did anyway, so what was the point?

She put the dirty nappy in a nappy sack, then carried it through to the bin, dropping it in. As she got into the hallway she saw that Ben was unlocking the front door.

She should have felt happy that he was back. He could do his magic thing and settle this tiny girl in milliseconds! But all she could feel was jealousy that he was coming to the rescue yet again.

'Why are you home?' she asked over Phoebe's crying.

He was hanging his coat on a hook. 'I spoke to Tom. Told him you were having a few difficulties and that I needed to spend a couple of days here.'

'What? You said *what*?'

Difficulties? He'd told their boss that she couldn't cope?

'It's not as bad as it sounds. I just told him things were difficult and both of us needed to be at home whilst Phoebe adjusted.'

He held out his hands, offering to take her, but Leah held on to Phoebe more tightly.

'You told Tom I wasn't coping?'

'Leah—'

She raised her hand to silence him. 'How *dare* you? How could you *do* that to me? Embarrass me in front of my boss? Criticise my parenting? I know you think I'm awful at this, but you don't have to tell the whole world! It's bad enough that you feel this way about me, but to start telling other people? People I respect?'

Ben stared at her. 'Leah, pass me Phoebe. Let me get her settled and then we can talk about this.'

'No! I don't want you here, acting all high and mighty, like you're the only one who can handle babies! How do you think it makes me feel if you step in every time I can't settle her? I want you to go. Phoebe isn't even your baby, so you don't get to take over with her—all right? *I'm* her mother! *I* am! And I will work this out and do it in my *own* way. I don't need you—so get out!'

He looked hurt. 'Leah!'

She marched past him and opened the front door. She glared at him. 'I can do this alone! But I'm not getting the *chance* to do this alone because you're always swooping in to the rescue! I know I came to the hospital, and I know I sought you out, and maybe I shouldn't have. But I'm not a helpless child and you're not my older brother, okay? Now, get out and don't come back unless I tell you to!'

Ben looked at her, hurt and surprise written all over his face. Inside, it was killing her. But what killed her more was his lack of belief in her. What she needed was love and support. Not criticism.

'But—'

'I mean it, Ben. *Go!*'

He swallowed hard and walked towards her. She

thought he was going to kiss her goodbye, but he didn't. He kissed Phoebe's wet cheek and stroked her baby daughter's back, and then he grabbed his coat and left.

She slammed the door shut behind him, determined not to cry any more.

But, oh, what had she done?

She patted Phoebe's back and bobbed her up and done, trying her best to soothe her ever-crying daughter.

'We'll be okay, you and me. You'll see…'

As Ben walked away down the path he almost stopped and turned around.

He would *not* let her do this to him! He was invested—his feelings were involved here, too! No, he'd not thought he wanted to be a dad at first, but he had come round to the idea. It had taken some time, but he felt ready. Ready to be a father not only to his son, but to Phoebe, too.

The time he'd already spent with her, cradling her in his arms, had been magical. He'd sat in that nursery, rocking her to sleep, looking down into her pretty little face with her button nose, and he'd fallen in love with her.

It had been easy.

But this…?

This wasn't.

He couldn't believe she'd kicked him out. But she'd been adamant. Hurt. Somehow he'd said the wrong thing when he'd only meant to help. That was all he'd ever done in his life. Stepped up to do what others couldn't.

There was no point in going back right now. He knew she wouldn't let him in. She probably wouldn't even open the door, and there was no way he was going to stand on her doorstep shouting. He didn't want to upset Phoebe.

And perhaps in the long run it would do Leah good? Perhaps she was right and she *did* need time alone to learn about Phoebe and work out how to deal with her? Phoebe was clearly a very vocal baby, and very happy to make it known when she wasn't content.

If he remembered correctly, when he had first started looking after his brother and sister he hadn't known what he was doing either. Had he cooked the chicken long enough or was he about to poison everyone? Was putting his baby sister in the bath after a particularly explosive nappy better than just cleaning her up with wipes? He'd learned how to test the temperature of the water safely. How to make sure he bought the special baby bath bubbles for her sensitive skin rather than use the one the rest of them used. How to know which cry meant what.

There had been a few weeks in the early days in which he'd made a right mess of everything—getting medication mixed up, giving antihistamines to one when he should have been giving them to another—but he'd got there in the end.

He could remember what that hopelessness had felt like. He'd never wanted to experience it again.

And yet here he was. Right back where he'd started. Hopeless and adrift.

He decided to head back to work. If Leah didn't need him, then he would go where he *was* needed. Tom would probably be surprised, but would no doubt be thrilled to have an extra pair of hands back.

His mood stayed dark for the rest of the day, and when home-time came around he went back to his own home with a heavy heart. Dragging his feet, knowing that this was not the place he wanted to be. This flat wasn't his home any more.

It hurt that she was shutting him out like this.

He wanted to be with his family.

He wanted to be with Leah and Phoebe and their son who was about to be born.

That was where his heart resided.

Leah felt her first Braxton Hicks contraction just after she'd finally got Phoebe off to sleep. It was almost as if Phoebe had sensed the turmoil of the day and realised how much Leah needed her to give her a break and not cry as much.

During Phoebe's first nap Leah had gone on the internet and looked at how getting a baby into a routine could help, and what she could do to soothe her child and induce relaxation. So that evening she'd given Phoebe a gentle, quiet bath in low lighting, gently singing lullabies, and once she'd towel-dried her she'd lain Phoebe on a soft fleecy blanket and given her a full body massage, having watched baby massage videos earlier in the day.

Phoebe had seemed to like it! And so had Leah! She had been able to relax for the first time in the presence of her baby, to enjoying her—enjoy her scent and her little noises and her cute little baby yawns as the massage began to take effect.

Continuing to sing softly, she had put Phoebe in a clean nappy, got her dressed in her softest onesie and then put her down to sleep in the crib, all drowsy. And Phoebe had gone to sleep without a single tear.

It was like a miracle! Leah was thrilled!

She wanted to tell someone, but the person she would usually turn to—Ben—wasn't here, because she'd told him to go.

She slumped on the sofa and briefly thought about ringing Sally.

But she didn't want Sally to know that she was struggling. Sally was such a brilliant mother. It had been so natural for her, and none of her own children had ever given her cause to lose it in any way, shape or form.

She sat thinking about that. About why it was so hard for her. She wondered if her problems had started because of Ben? She'd been so tense, so worried about him not accepting Phoebe, and perhaps that fear had passed to Phoebe and she had sensed it? And then Leah had felt all that resentment about Ben swooping in and taking Phoebe from her. Being the super-father who could do no wrong when it had been *her* baby and *her* time and they'd not had a proper moment to bond.

Perhaps there was nothing wrong with Phoebe at all. Perhaps it was all down to her picking up on Leah's apprehension. A baby needed to feel secure with its mother, and all Phoebe could sense from *her* mother was fear. Fear that Ben wouldn't accept Phoebe. Fear that he would hate being a father. Fear that he would leave.

Well, he hadn't left. She'd kicked him out. And, though it had felt terrible to do it, hadn't today been much better with Phoebe?

It had almost been a breeze, because Leah had been much more relaxed. She hadn't felt as if the Sword of Damocles was above her head at all times. She hadn't been waiting for the axe to fall. And though she felt terribly lonely, with no one to talk to, this was simply how it would have been in her original plan—before Ben had come along with his one-night stand and his super-sperm and made everything complicated.

And that was when she realised it was all *his* fault. It had all gone wrong when *he'd* become involved! She'd been *fine* before him!

Leah rubbed at her belly, waiting for the tightness to release and go. She would make a cup of tea. She would put her feet up for a moment. She would enjoy being single once again.

But when she sat down with her mug of tea and switched on the television, the sound low, she didn't sit staring at the screen. She found herself looking across at the seat where Ben always sat, wondering what he was doing.

And if he felt as miserable as she did...

CHAPTER THIRTEEN

BEN SAT STARING into space, his mind in some far-off place as all around him the A&E department thrummed with activity.

He hadn't seen Leah for a week, and despite his numerous attempts to contact her she wouldn't pick up the phone and she didn't answer the door to her flat.

All he wanted was a chance to explain, but she seemed determined to shut him out and he couldn't comprehend that. He needed to know how she was doing! She was carrying his child and he had a right to know how she was. And he missed Phoebe. He wanted to see her, too, and know that she was okay. Not that he doubted Leah and her ability to care for her. Not at all. He trusted her completely.

He was contemplating sitting on her doorstep and not moving until she had to come out for food, or answer the door for a parcel—*something*—when Richard came to his side.

'There's someone asking specifically for you.'

Ben continued to stare, lost in thought.

'Mate? Ben?' Richard gave him a nudge.

'What? Sorry.'

'You were away with the fairies, there. Penny for them?'

Ben shook his head. 'You don't want them, believe me.'

'Still no word from Leah?'

'No.'

'She'll come round. They always do. Women are essentially pressure cookers. They let stuff build up and build up and they say nothing—and then *bam!* Out it all comes, at toxic levels, and all you can do is let them say it all and allow them to cool down. Then you can approach safely.' He smiled. 'Good metaphor, eh?'

Ben smiled. 'You sound like you have experience in these matters.'

'Three sisters, mate.'

'I have one.'

'So you know! Come on—there's a woman asking for you in cubicle four.'

'Who is she?'

Richard passed him the triage chart. 'Sally Lombard.'

Ben stood up, his eyes scanning the triage notes with concern. Query broken wrist. 'Right, thanks. I'll get straight on it.'

Richard nodded and left him to it.

Ben stood up and sucked in a deep breath. Sally Lombard was Leah's best friend. She might know how she was getting on. He hoped she'd asked for him specifically to let him know. Though would she even know that Leah had kicked him out? Was she here to tell him to stay away? Or to sort it out?

With apprehension, he walked into Minors and opened the curtain to cubicle four. 'Sally! It's good to see you again. I'm sorry to hear you're hurt. Have you had any painkillers?'

She smiled at him. 'Thanks. You, too. I've had some paracetamol. It was stupid. I fell on my wrist, tripping over the damned cat.'

'You own a cat?'

'Sure. Don't you have any pets?'

'No.'

'Kids love animals. Just you wait—you'll have a houseful soon.'

He smiled, glad that she seemed to think that he would still be with Leah. 'What did you fall on to? Concrete? Wooden floor?'

'Parquet flooring. I was carrying a basket of ironing to take upstairs and the damned cat snaked its way through my legs and I tripped.' She held out her wrist for him to examine.

Ben could see there was a smallish bruise forming. It might be broken if it had taken the full force of the fall. 'Did you bang your head?'

'No.'

'You didn't pass out? You didn't feel dizzy?'

'No.'

'Not even before you fell?'

'No.'

He examined her hand, checking that she could feel him touching the sides of her fingers, whether she could move her fingers and the wrist, whether she could make a fist. She could—but everything hurt.

'We'll probably need to get an X-ray, but I'm sure you've more than likely sprained it.'

Sally nodded.

'You've come alone today?' he asked.

'Hubby's at home with the kids. And, no, I don't have Leah waiting for me in the waiting room.'

Ben looked down and away. So she *did* know. 'How is she? Do you know?'

'Of course I know.' She smiled.

'And?'

'You have to understand, Ben, she's my friend. My

best friend. And if I'm going to be in anyone's corner here it's going to be hers. But...'

He looked up. 'But?'

Sally let out a breath. 'She's trying to pretend that everything's all right. And it is! Phoebe is a crier. Some babies just *are*. It doesn't mean there's anything wrong, or that she's being a bad mother. Some babies just cry a lot—they like to be held, to be in contact with someone all the time.'

'But?' he said again.

Sally let out a resigned sigh. 'I can see she's struggling. She hasn't said anything to me, but I popped round the other day to see how she was and she looked on the verge of tears the whole time. It's hard with the baby due soon, too.'

Ben nodded. He could imagine.

'She told me she'd sent you packing. That you'd said something about her not coping. Please tell me you didn't say that?'

'I didn't. Well, not exactly...'

'*Ben!* You know how much being a good mother means to her! To have the person you love tell you that maybe you aren't coping is—'

'She loves me?'

Sally gave him a look that said, *What do you think?* 'You need to talk to her. Tell her that she's doing a brilliant job, that she's a brilliant mother and she's doing everything right. She needs to hear that from you.'

He shook his head. 'She doesn't want to hear anything from me. She made that quite clear.'

'You don't have time for your ego to get in the way of things right now. You don't have time to feel hurt because she kicked you out. She's heavily pregnant, filled with raging hormones and she's scared. And you, God help us, are the only person apart from me who makes her feel safe!'

Ben stared at Sally, wanting to make everything right there and then, but knowing it was impossible. He was at work. He had a job to do.

'I'll arrange your X-ray. Wait here.'

He headed off to the desk to write out the form and sat there, his mind whirling with millions of thoughts.

Leah loved him? He knew he loved *her*, but neither of them had said it out loud. And she'd thrown him out! Did she really need to hear from him? He wasn't sure anything he said would change her mind.

But it would be good to try and see the baby. It had taken a lot of internal adjustment for him to decide he was going to love Phoebe as much as his own son, and he wanted to see her and hold her again.

He had that right! Even though the little girl wasn't his own flesh and blood, it didn't matter. Biology didn't make a father. Fathers were made from those who stayed, no matter what, through thick and thin.

Leah had taken Phoebe to her GP and got her checked out at the baby clinic and had her weighed. Everyone kept saying that she had a healthy baby, and that it was just a case of them getting to know one another—that was all. That maybe Phoebe could sense a lack of confidence in her mother…

It was something that had preyed on her mind, so she'd taken Phoebe on a long, long walk—one that had left her with backache. But she hadn't worried about that. Instead she'd given herself a firm talking-to, settling her mind, telling herself where she'd been going wrong with Phoebe and that all she needed to do was relax when she was with her daughter and not be on this knife-edge, straining for perfection all the time.

Becoming a parent was a learning curve. No one got it right straight away. *No one!* She'd been putting undue pressure on herself and look what had happened!

And now she'd returned home, hauling the pushchair over the step to get into the flat and leaving Phoebe to sleep whilst she rested and had a cup of tea.

All she wanted—all she had ever wanted—was to have a happy family. The pressure she had put on herself to get that dream had been enormous, and as soon as Phoebe had begun crying it had destroyed the image in her head of what it was supposed to have been. And since then Leah had been desperately trying to claw it back, getting more and more frantic, the further and further it slipped away.

And what else had she done? She'd blamed Ben for it. She'd not blamed herself—she'd blamed him. She'd accused him of taking her dream, of being the super-parent who could solve any problem.

But it hadn't been his fault at all! So he had more experience looking after kids than she had? How was that *his* fault?

And she missed him. Missed him so much!

It hurt not having him with her. She had got used to him being by her side, at work and at home. Whenever she had a funny story to tell, or just wanted to tell someone about her day, she turned to Ben—and he wasn't there any more.

It killed her not to answer the phone to him. Not to text him. Not to show up at work, or at his home. And that just made her want to cry, because his home ought to be with *them*! With his family. With Phoebe. With their son, when he arrived.

Why had she held back for so long? To prove to herself that she could do this alone? That she didn't need him? That because she'd only ever relied on herself for her entire life admitting to needing someone else was some sort of weakness?

She was beginning to think that that was a lie. Being able to admit that you needed someone was a *strength*, because it meant that you knew yourself and knew your own limits, and knew that by needing someone else you could only be stronger than you were before because there were two of you!

But she'd been afraid to call him back. Afraid to apologise. Because what if she'd ruined it?

She loved him. It was as simple as that. And she missed him. Missed his smile and his warmth and the way he'd sit on the end of the couch and absently rub her feet. The way she'd wake to find him wrapped around her, feeling safe and secure.

The way he made her feel.

Loved.

Phoebe would benefit from him being here, too. And their son, when he got here.

So enough of this nonsense!

She got to her feet and went into the hall to put on some shoes and her coat. Then she scooped up Phoebe and got her ready to go out, too.

'We're going to get Daddy. Yes, we are! And Daddy is going to come home with us, if he can find it within himself to forgive me. Because your mummy has been pretty silly these last few days, Phoebe. But I guess you'd know that, having watched me be an idiot ever since you met me.'

Leah grabbed her keys and opened the front door—

only to stand there in astonishment at seeing Ben there, his hand raised, about to knock.

'Ben!'

He smiled uncertainly at her. 'Hi.' He looked at Phoebe. 'May I come in?'

And that was when a flush of water hit the front step.

Leah looked down in surprise, then looked up at him. 'My waters have broken!'

'Let me take Phoebe.' Ben stepped forward and took Phoebe from Leah's arms. 'We need to get you to hospital.'

She nodded, still in shock—unable, it seemed, to form words. It was early. Six weeks early. She was only thirty-four weeks pregnant!

'Have you packed a hospital bag?'

She just looked at Ben and shook her head. She'd thought she had plenty of time to do that. In fact, she'd thought she might do it next week, or the week after that. After she'd had a bit more time with Phoebe to settle in.

'Then let's get you a towel to sit on in the car.'

'Y-yes. Okay.' She waddled back inside and grabbed a towel from the cupboard.

This was it. She would give birth today. Or would the midwives try to stop her labour? Would they do that after the loss of her waters? She tried to think back to the days when she'd done a rotation on Labour and Delivery, but she couldn't think clearly.

By the time she got back to her doorstep Ben had got baby Phoebe strapped inside her car seat, and he ran up the steps to take her arm and help her down the path.

'Ben, I'm scared.'

'Don't be. I've got you.'

'What if it all goes wrong? What if something happens to the baby?'

'Nothing's going to happen.'

'You don't know that.'

'And neither do you. Let's not worry about something until it happens.'

He helped her lower herself into the front passenger seat and then ran around the front of the car, got in and gunned the engine.

'Drive carefully.'

'I always do.'

'I know. I...' She looked at him. 'I'm sorry for what I did. Throwing you out. I didn't mean to... I was just... scared.'

'It's okay.'

'No, it's not. I was mean and I took it out on you. Blaming you. For everything. I realise now that that was wrong, and I feel very embarrassed about that. I had a dream, you see, and it was all going wrong. And I couldn't understand why, when I'd dreamt about it for so long. And in my head I somehow thought that the only anomaly in my imagined future was that *you* were there. You were interfering with it and stopping me from bonding with my daughter.'

He looked at her. '*Our* daughter.'

She smiled. 'Yes. Our daughter.' She reached out and placed her hand on his. 'I'm so sorry! I've missed you so much!'

He grabbed her hand to squeeze her fingers. 'It's okay.'

'You forgive me?'

'Of course I do! I could never be angry with you. You're everything to me. But I need to say I'm sorry, too. For making you think I gave our boss the impression that you weren't coping. I should never had said anything negative about your parenting. You're a brilliant mum. We're all learning about each other. This is new ground for us.'

Ben glanced at Phoebe through the rearview mirror, asleep in her car seat. Peaceful. Content.

'She's not crying.'

Leah smiled, then grimaced. 'I might, though.' She gripped her belly and groaned slightly, leaning forward in pain.

'Contraction?'

She nodded, unable to speak.

'Try to time it.'

'I'll try.' She groaned again as the car pulled to a stop by a red light.

'Let's talk about something good. Something positive. Take your mind off the pain.'

'Like what?'

'Like...' He turned to face her in the car. 'Like I love you.'

She gasped, her face lighting up in surprise. 'What?'

'I love you, Leah Hudson, and I want to be with you for ever.'

She laughed. Pure joy and shock. 'I love you, too.'

He beamed a smile back. 'So...does that mean I can move in?'

Behind them they heard the irate beep of a car horn and Ben glanced forward and noticed the light was green. He began driving again.

'You're sure?' asked Leah.

He grabbed her hand and kissed the back of it. 'Of course I'm sure.'

'You're not just saying this because I'm about to have your baby?'

'I'd be asking you if I could move in if you were eighty years old, smelly and lived with twenty cats.' He smiled.

She smiled back. 'I've always preferred dogs.' Then she groaned again as another contraction hit.

Ben helped her breathe through it. 'You're doing great. That's it—nice long, slow breaths. So?'

'So?'

'*Can* I move in?'

She laughed with joy, then nodded. 'Yes! Of course you can! I'd love it. We all would.'

It took him another twenty minutes in the heavy traffic to get to the hospital, and by the time he pulled up in the drop-off zone outside Maternity Leah was clearly in great discomfort and complaining that she felt like pushing.

'Try not to,' said Ben.

'I can't stop myself!'

'Aren't first labours meant to be long?' he asked as he ran inside to get a wheelchair.

Leah wished she could answer him, but another contraction had hit and this time she *had* to push. There was just no stopping it. It was completely involuntary—as if her body knew what needed to happen next and no amount of stalling was going to stop it from happening.

'Ben!' she screamed as he emerged from the hospital with a wheelchair and—thank heavens—a midwife who was pulling on a set of gloves. 'I can't help it! I had to push!'

'Hello, my lovely. I'm Carla and I'm a midwife and we need to get you into this chair. Can you get out of the car for me?'

Leah struggled to move, but she felt like a beached whale—immovable and stuck in a weird position that didn't seem to hurt as much as others.

With a lot of adjustment, a lot of encouragement and

two sets of helping hands, Leah was finally pulled from the front seat into the wheelchair and rushed inside the hospital. Ben followed behind, baby Phoebe in his arms.

She didn't recall much of the mad rush through the corridors. Her eyes were closed for most of it as she breathed and panted and pushed whenever a contraction hit. Then suddenly they were in a room and she was being helped onto a bed.

'I'll need to examine you, Leah. Can I remove your jeans?'

She nodded quickly, groaning as her damp jeans were slid down her legs. Carla took one look and nodded with a smile on her face. 'I can see the head.'

'What? Already? I'm only thirty-four weeks—this is too soon!'

'Well, nothing's stopping this little one from making its appearance today, so let's get down to business.'

Ben gripped her hand as Carla coached her through her breathing and told her how and when to push.

She groaned and gasped and made noises she'd never heard herself make before as wave after wave of contractions surged through her body. How could she take so much pain? Where would she find the endurance?

But every time she wanted to quit Ben told her that she could carry on. That she could *do* this!

'Come on, Leah, he's nearly here! One more contraction—that's all!'

Carla told her to pant as the head crowned and emerged, and Leah glanced down to see a shock of dark hair.

She gasped with joy. 'Oh, my God!'

'One more push, Leah. The next contraction and he's out!'

'Okay...' She nodded.

Ben looked directly into her eyes. 'Forget moving in. I want to marry you. Will you do me the honour of becoming my wife?'

She gripped his hand in hers, gazing lovingly into his eyes. 'Yes! I will!'

And with one final push she brought their son into the world.

And there was a new voice, a new presence, a new love formed within their hearts.

EPILOGUE

'THERE! THAT'S THE last of the boxes.' Ben stood up and rubbed the small of his back. He'd been packing and lifting boxes all week, and now that they had moved into their new home it was time to start unpacking them all over again!

Leah passed him a mug of tea. 'Well, I found the kettle—that's the most important thing when you move house.'

He sipped his drink. 'No, it's not.'

'No?'

He put the mug down and wrapped his arms around his wife. 'No. It's you and Noah and Phoebe. *You're* the most important things.'

He was about to kiss her when Sally came in, holding Phoebe's hand and tugging Noah along as they both toddled beside her.

'Get a room, you two! There are children present.'

They both laughed and scooped up a child each. Ben took his daughter and Leah took their son.

'Have you had the tour, Sal?' asked Leah.

'Course! It's beautiful! I'm totally jealous!'

'Thanks for looking after the kids last night.'

'No problem. You can call me any time—you know that, right?' She popped a kiss on the head of each child and then her eyes widened. 'Oh, my God, I totally forgot your housewarming gift! I left it in the car—hang on!' She dashed back outside.

Ben and Leah kissed and hugged their children, and then took them through to the back garden. It was a child's dream. Large and grassy, with a Wendy house and a toy slide and, further down the lawn, an old gnarly tree with a tree house for when they were a little older.

Phoebe squirmed to get out of her father's arms so she could toddle off and play, and Noah set off, too, to try and catch up with his older sister. Older by two weeks!

Ben put his arm around his wife. 'Happy?'

'Mmm… Yes. Are you?'

'I'm in paradise.'

He leant in to give her a kiss, trying to enjoy this brief moment of calm. This brief moment when the kids were giggling and tumbling along in the grass, falling over as they bent to try and pick daisies, watching in fascination as butterflies fluttered by.

He knew there was still the rest of the house to unbox. Furniture to heft and move. A kitchen to arrange. But for now everything was perfect. Just as it should be.

Had either of them ever imagined a future as wonderful as this? Had either of them ever believed that this happiness could exist?

At that moment Sally came out to join them, carrying a large cardboard box that very suspiciously had holes in the top.

Ben frowned. 'What's this?'

'Open it!'

Leah called Phoebe and Noah over to join them on the grass as she untied the bow that held the box together and flipped open the cardboard flaps.

A golden head of fur with gorgeous brown eyes looked out at them all and barked.

'Oh, my God! A puppy! What breed is it?'

'Golden retriever.'

'Sally, this must have set you back a fortune!'

Leah watched delightedly as the puppy stumbled from the box and began to excitedly sniff the grass. Noah and Phoebe squealed happily.

'My brother-in-law breeds them, so I got a freebie. You said you wanted a dog.'

They had. And it was the perfect family set-up, wasn't it? A great family, a wonderful home, perfect children. A dog.

'It's a she, by the way.'

'She's gorgeous! She's perfect! Thank you.' Ben gave Sally a hug.

They'd talked about getting a dog for the kids. It was something he'd always wanted as a child.

'So, what are you going to call her?'

Ben knelt down to ruffle the dog's fur—and then fell over as the dog excitedly jumped up at his lap. He laughed and rolled in the grass.

Leah looked down at them all. Her husband, her two children, her dog…

Life just didn't get any better than this.

* * * * *

MILLS & BOON

Coming next month

ISLAND DOCTOR TO ROYAL BRIDE?
Scarlet Wilson

'What do you think of Corinez so far?' She could hear the edge of uncertainty in his voice.

She took a step closer and put her hand on his arm. From here she could smell his aftershave, see the shadow starting to show along his jawline. 'I like it,' she replied honestly. 'And I want to find out more.' She licked her lips and moved even closer. 'And I like it even more that I can see how passionate you are about your country, and how much you want to make things better.'

He looked down at her, his hand sliding behind her waist. 'That's exactly how you are about Temur Sapora.' He lowered his head so his lips were only inches from hers. His breath warmed her skin, 'Maybe it makes us a good match.'

'Maybe it does,' she agreed as she moved closer until her lips were only millimetres from his. She couldn't help but smile.

'I sense you might be trouble,' he teased.

'I think you might be right.' She smiled as his lips met hers. Every cell in her body started reacting. All she cared about was this moment. Her body melded to his. She was already tired and somehow leaning against him made her instincts soar.

She didn't even notice when the elevator doors slid open.

What she did notice was someone clearing their throat. Loudly.

They sprang apart and Philippe stiffened. 'Luka.' He nodded to the dark-suited man at the door. 'You're looking for me?'

The man started talking in a low voice, his eyes darting over to Arissa and giving her the most dismissive of glances. She was instantly uncomfortable. She waited a few seconds then slid out of the elevator before the doors closed again and started walking down the corridor, praying she was heading in the right direction.

Her heart was thrumming against her chest, part from the reaction to Philippe and part from the adrenaline coursing through her body in annoyance.

She turned a corner and sighed in relief as she recognised the corridor, finding her room quickly and closing the door behind her. She took off her jacket and shoes and flung herself down on the bed. Her head was spinning.

Last time she'd kissed him he was just Philippe, the doctor who was helping at the clinic. This time she'd kissed Prince Philippe of Corinez. Did it feel different? Her heart told her no, but her brain couldn't quite decide. And as she closed her eyes, she still wasn't quite sure.

Continue reading
ISLAND DOCTOR TO ROYAL BRIDE?
Scarlet Wilson

Available next month
www.millsandboon.co.uk

COMING SOON!

We really hope you enjoyed reading this book. If you're looking for more romance, be sure to head to the shops when new books are available on

Thursday 24th January

To see which titles are coming soon, please visit

millsandboon.co.uk/nextmonth

LET'S TALK

Romance

For exclusive extracts, competitions
and special offers, find us online:

f facebook.com/millsandboon

🐦 @MillsandBoon

📷 @MillsandBoonUK

Get in touch on 01413 063232

For all the latest titles coming soon, visit
millsandboon.co.uk/nextmonth